RICHARD, ROSE AND
MRS. BEEWATER

RICHARD, ROSE
AND
MRS. BEEWATER

by
J. K. STUNT

VICTORY PRESS
EASTBOURNE

ISBN 0 85476 225 6

Printed in Great Britain for
VICTORY PRESS (Evangelical Publishers Ltd.),
Lottbridge Drove, Eastbourne, Sussex,
by Richard Clay (The Chaucer Press) Ltd.,
Bungay, Suffolk.

CHAPTER 1

It was the dog on the common who really introduced them. Rose loved him. She called him Chuffy because she did not know what his name was, nor to whom he belonged, nor even exactly where he lived though she guessed it must be in one of the houses which fringed the common. Most of the day he just sat on the grass opposite the house where Richard and Rose lived or else he wandered about by himself, barking a little every now and then. He was very careful never to go on the road where cars and lorries were apt to swing round the corner at rather a high speed. Rose liked to think he had given himself the job of keeping watch on all that was going on.

One day during the Easter school holidays it happened that Rose was alone, Richard having gone to the dentist. Chuffy, as usual, took no notice of her but allowed himself to be patted and stroked while going on with his job of keeping watch.

"What are you looking at, silly?" Rose asked him. Then she became aware that someone had stopped beside her: an old lady, but not in the least like some people's idea of an old lady; no shawls or mufflers or string bags; there was nothing old-fashioned about her although you could see that she was old. She had a sprightly look. She was very carefully dressed and her hair was very beautifully done under a smart little hat. Her eyes were blue and clear and she had a delicate complexion.

"Is that your dog?" she said to Rose.

Rose stood up. "No. I don't know who he belongs to. But he's always here."

"Yes, I'd noticed that. What is his name?"

"I call him Chuffy. He has a medal on his collar but the writing is all worn off. He looks like Chuffy, doesn't he?"

"Ye-es. Or Scruffy!"

"He's not Scruffy!" said Rose indignantly, giving him another fervent hug. There was something, however, in what the old lady said: though he didn't look neglected his gingery hair was rather long and fell over his eyes, and his tail was a bit feathery. He had white paws though and a white patch under his chin where the hair was soft and silky.

"Well, Chuffy or Scruffy. What is *your* name?"

"Rose."

"I've seen you before, I think."

"Have you," returned Rose, indifferently.

"You live here, don't you?"

Rose nodded and pointed at the tall London house across the road. She turned as though to go back to it but there was nothing to go back for until Ricky returned. Her mother, as always on a week day, was away running her business, and Mrs. Mumford, the daily who did everything in the house, would not at this time in the morning want Rose 'under her feet' as she called it. It was too early for elevenses.

The old lady started to walk on. Then she looked back at Rose. "Coming?"

"Where?" asked Rose.

"I'm just going to the shops. I don't go very far from here these days." And she sighed. Rose, walking beside her, and having given her one or two long looks, thought perhaps she liked her. "Do you live here too?"

"Yes. Over there, on the common, not far from you. I do now at least, but it's not my home. I am staying with my daughter, Mrs. Steele. I used to live in Kensington. And before that in India, and before that in Rhodesia and Kenya. All over the place. In fact, anywhere but in the wilds of South West London." She sighed again.

Rose digested this in silence while they walked on and presently came to a little, quiet street full of small shops.

"Would you like an ice-cream?" the old lady asked suddenly.

Rose, privately, thought it was rather early in the day for ices but answered politely, "Yes, if you will have one too." Then as she saw fumblings going on in a handbag, said, "I've plenty of money. You don't need to pay for me."

"You rude little thing," said the old lady briefly.

Rose looked at her. "I'm not being rude. I simply said I'd plenty of money. I'll pay for yours too," said Rose. "If you like," she added, seeing the pink flush which had risen to her companion's cheeks.

"Very well then! You can pay for mine too. *I* have *not* got much money; far too little to spend on little girls who don't want it!" And, her eyes sparkling angrily, but with a great deal of dignity for such a small person, she swept into a shop which displayed bread, a few buns and some jars of sweets in its window. "Two ice-creams, please," she said to the pleasant-faced woman behind the counter, who evidently knew her well, and she sat down, still with dignity, at one of two or three small tables in a rather dingy room at the back of the shop. Rose had imagined herself licking a cone or sucking a lolly walking through the street, but she now realised that with her new acquaintance such a thing would be impossible. Old ladies such as this old lady obviously didn't eat things in streets!

The woman brought two little mounds of ice-cream on two little glass dishes. "Like a biscuit with it, dear?"

"She's a very kind person," the old lady said in a low voice, when, the biscuits having arrived on a thick yellow plate, she started delicately on her ice, "but I do wish she wouldn't call me 'dear'. They all do it here, or if it isn't 'dear' it's 'love'."

"Or 'duck'," volunteered Rose.

"Or 'duck', as you say."

"Perhaps she doesn't know your name."

"In Kensington she would have called me 'Madam'."

"What is your name?"

"Mrs. Beewater. B-E-E-W-A-T-E-R."

Rose gurgled with laughter. "What a queer name! But I *love* it! Beewater. It sounds like a lovely summer day and a clear blue lake and a bumble-bee zooming along like they do when it's hot and all the birds are singing. I've never met anybody with that name before."

"It's a very well-known name—in certain circles, that is to say." Not, she implied, in South West London. "My husband was a great civil engineer. He made wonderful roads all over the world."

Rose thought this over. "Is your husband dead or are you divorced?"

"Dear me, what a very odd child you are! No. My husband and I were *not* divorced. He died five years ago."

"My father and mother are divorced. But she's married again."

"I see," said Mrs. Beewater, thinking that that explained a lot.

Spooning up the last of her ice Rose said, "Did you say your daughter's name is Mrs. Steele? Jennifer and Marilyn Steele live somewhere on the common."

"My granddaughters. Do you know them?"

Rose nodded. "One of them is in my form at school."

"At St. Leonid's? Well, how interesting. You must come to tea one day."

Rose made no reply to this. She had no use for the two Steele girls: they were to her quite, quite uninteresting. Again Mrs. Beewater looked at her sharply. When she was young one would have said, Thank you very much, when invited to tea, but this time she did not comment. Instead she asked, "Have you any brothers and sisters?"

"A brother. Ricky. Richard's his real name."

"So it's just you two and your mother at home."

"No, I told you. Mummy married again. Jack's there.

Jack is her husband."

"I see," said Mrs. Beewater.

"And you couldn't call Mummy 'at home' really. Not really."

"Doesn't she live there?"

"Oh, yes. She lives there. But she's always out. During the week, I mean. She's Managing Director of Elwyn Gowns Limited—you know—shops all over the place."

"And what does your—her—I mean Jack, do?"

"Oh, I don't know. Some office or other. He's out too but usually he comes home earlier than Mummy does."

"So who looks after you and Ricky?"

Rose stared. "No one looks after us. We don't need looking after."

"Well, the cooking and the shopping and the house cleaning and everything."

"Mrs. Mumford does that. She comes in every day. She's been with us years and *years*. Well, I'm nine now and she came first when I was only six. That was after Daddy went (he's married again too, by the way) and we lived in another house then, and when we moved over here Mrs. Mumford came with us." Rose began to giggle. "We call her Mum. So it's rather awkward sometimes. When we're talking about her and Mummy people never know which is which, Mummy or Mum!"

"And you like this Mrs. Mumford, do you?"

"She's all right," said Rose.

When they left the little shop the woman at the counter smiled cheerfully and said, "Bye bye till next time", to which Mrs. Beewater responded gracefully, "Good morning."

The two walked up the street together. "I have to go into the post office," said Mrs. Beewater. She was there quite a few minutes, and having bought her stamps and a packet of envelopes, she was quite astonished to see Rose still outside. Rose was a thin child with long, slim legs which looked even longer in her close-fitting jeans. She had straight, tumbling, yellow hair and a pale face. Her nose and mouth were well-shaped and she had good eyes —deep, large, grey eyes which looked gravely out on the world. What a plain child, thought Mrs. Beewater, and then as Rose smiled at her, but what a lovely smile she has. She ought to smile more often.

"You didn't expect me to wait for you, did you?" Rose said.

"I'm very glad you did," replied Mrs. Beewater. They took the road towards the common and there, coming across the grass from the wide main road where the buses ran, was Richard.

"My brother," said Rose rather shyly. "That's Richard coming towards us," and again that rare smile lit up her usually grave face.

Richard was tall for his age (he was two years older than Rose), slim like his sister and good-looking. He was indeed a handsome boy and when he liked could be very charming. After Rose's introduction he and Mrs. Beewater greeted each other and Mrs. Beewater then went on her way.

"*Who* did you say she was?" asked Richard as they walked home.

'Mrs. Beewater,' said Rose possessively, as if this acquaintance of less than two hours' standing were an old friend from her long lost past.

"I know. You said. Funny name anyway. But who is she?"

"Well, I don't know really," Rose had to confess. "Yes, I do though. She's the grandmother of Jennifer and Marilyn at school."

"Huh!"

"Yes, I know. They're awful. But she's not."

"How d'you know?"

"I just know. She gave me an ice—well, actually I gave her one because she said she hadn't any money, or not much. Ricky, isn't it awful a person that age not having any money."

"She didn't look as if she hadn't any," said Richard thoughtfully. "Perhaps she had some really and didn't want to spend it."

Rose shook her head. "No. It wasn't like that at all." She remembered apologetically having boasted of her own riches and how Mrs. Beewater hadn't liked it; but she hadn't meant to boast, she'd simply been saying what was true.

"I don't think she's very happy. She doesn't like living here."

"She doesn't have to."

"Perhaps she does. Perhaps she hasn't anywhere else to live."

"Where did you pick her up?"

"I was just talking to Chuffy and she came along."

"Out of the blue."

"Yes."

Richard looked at his wrist watch. "Do you suppose Mum would give us some cocoa now? I say, you didn't ask me how I got on at the dentist's."

"How did you?"

"All right. He didn't hurt much. But he might have. And you didn't ask."

'Sorry," said Rose contritely. Her head was full of Mrs. Beewater.

CHAPTER 2

That evening while Mrs. Beewater sat at dinner with her daughter and son-in-law (Jennifer and Marilyn having had milk and biscuits in the kitchen had gone up to bed) she told them about Rose: Rose Anders and her brother Richard who lived just across the common.

"A most surprising child," she said. "I've seen her once or twice on the common, but today I spoke to her."

"Really," said Robert Steele. He had scarcely heard what was said, but one had to be polite to one's mother-in-law even though one was a very busy man who was always having to think of several things at once.

"Is she one of that terrible family whose father went to prison recently?" enquired Margaret Steele.

"Indeed not," said Mrs. Beewater, adding after a pause, "She goes to school with Jennifer and Marilyn."

Margaret Steele wrinkled her forehead, and said, "Rose *Anders*? I don't know the name."

"She says her mother runs a dress shop and is divorced from the father."

"You know who that is," said Robert Steele, looking at his wife. "Hilda Runnall. Married Jack Runnall—remember? About two, perhaps three, years ago."

"*Oh*," said Margaret Steele, pursing her lips. "Yes, now I know the child you mean. Rose Anders, of course. Yes, I should think she would be 'surprising' as you call it. I am not anxious for Jennifer and Marilyn to have too much to do with her."

"I shouldn't think she wants too much to do with them," said Mrs. Beewater, a little acidly.

Mrs. Steele put down her knife and fork abruptly. "And what exactly do you mean by that?"

"Only, dear, that they are entirely different."

"As you say, they are entirely different! I sit with Mrs. Runnall on the S.S.C. Committee." (Margaret sat on so many committees that her mother had long ago given up trying to remember what they were all about.) "And I can only deplore the way she brings up her children. In fact, she does not bring them up. They just run wild while she is out all day looking after her shops. Such a woman ought not to have children."

"Elwyn Gowns Limited," said Mr. Steele thoughtfully. "She must be making a packet, beside what he earns."

"Do you mean Jack?" enquired Mrs. Beewater.

"Really, Mother! Must you call him by his Christian name?"

"The child called him Jack and I didn't know his surname."

"Then that just proves they are not being brought up properly. Please don't encourage Jennifer and Marilyn to have anything to do with them."

"I certainly shall not," said Mrs. Beewater, placidly eating turbot. "But I scarcely think their influence will be bad for me and I intend to see more of Rose. An interesting and unusual child. You could be right though about her mother and her lack of bringing up. I don't think Rose is very happy."

The next morning Mrs. Beewater took another walk across the common past the house where Rose lived. Chuffy, the dog, was in his usual place, sitting bolt upright, watching, not missing anything but paying no heed to passers-by. Rose was not there however. Mrs. Beewater looked up at the tall house across the road, noting its well-kept condition, the freshness of the paint, the cleanness of the windows, the fresh net curtains and the small paved garden in front with its tubs full of flowers. Mrs. Beewater had an eye for such details.

She walked sadly on. Perhaps she is looking out of the window, she thought, and saw me coming but doesn't want to meet me again. After all, why should she? I am seventy years older than she!

She need not have worried. At that very minute Rose would have been happy to be on her own familiar common with Mrs. Beewater and Chuffy rather than in the West End with her mother and brother, being made to try on new clothes in preparation for the summer term at school. Hilda Runnall had had that morning one of her rare bouts of remembering the needs of her children and had whisked them up to town in spite of their protests.

"You can't say I often make you do things," she had told them good-humouredly, "so just this once you must put up with it. And go and put on a dress, Rose, instead of those everlasting jeans. You look a sight."

"I don't care how I look," said Rose rebelliously.

"So it seems," her mother agreed. "Ricky, change your shoes. It must be six months since you've cleaned those."

"I haven't any others," said Ricky. "Honest, I haven't. Mum threw the old ones away."

"Nonsense!" said Hilda briskly. "Oh—well, did she? Then we must get shoes too. Mum, where are you? Just give a brush to Ricky's shoes, would you? Now hurry, children; we must go, and I haven't got time to waste."

Mrs. Runnall was tall with a beautiful, large figure—a wonderful figure for clothes. Her blonde hair was straight and shining and smooth, drawn back into an imposing bun. She was an imposing woman. Rose and Ricky admired her very much, but, secretly, Rose wished she was a bit more like other people's mothers. You couldn't imagine her, for instance, sitting on your bed at night listening to you or telling you a story, certainly not cuddling you or even kissing you. She wasn't made that way. Not that she was unkind: she was never unkind; it was just that you could never get near her.

To look at, Richard was very much like his mother. He

was tall for eleven, and straight backed, and he had his mother's wide forehead and broad nose. Rose thought quite often he was like her in his ways too; there were days when he seemed a long way off, remote like a snow-covered mountain. But in spite of this Ricky was her dear friend and companion and there wasn't anything in the world she wouldn't do for him.

"Come along, Rose," called Mrs. Runnall. "I'm going out to the car. The children will be back to lunch, Mum. Or no, perhaps they won't. Do you want to have lunch out, Ricky?"

"I don't mind."

"Well, if you and Rose do come in you can have a rasher or something. It doesn't matter."

Rose came sulkily down the stairs in a pinky dress which had once been pretty, and in the hall Mum seized her and ran an old comb through her hair. "You look like an old mop!" she said. "Them yellow hairs of yours would look lovely if you brushed them. Who's going to marry you if you don't take a pride in yourself?"

"If they don't want to marry me they needn't!" said Rose, and wrenching herself free she ran out to the car. All three sat in the front of the large Humber, with Rose in the middle. In a way it was rather fun to be going out somewhere, the three of them together, although it wouldn't be much fun trying on clothes. "Will you come and have lunch with us, Mummy?"

"Oh, I shouldn't think so, Rose. No, I shan't have time." With one hand on the steering-wheel she fumbled with the other in her handbag and produced a couple of pound notes which she passed to Ricky. "There. Find somewhere nice and give Rose a good lunch. Now let's talk about what we're going to buy."

The rest of the morning was spent on clothes. Richard didn't mind it particularly but Rose positively hated it. She loathed being hauled in and out of dresses and told to "Stand there", "Turn round", "Look in the glass" and

"Stay *still*, Rose!" But at last the ordeal was over and they were free, with no responsibility for the piles and piles of clothes which would in due course be delivered at the house, to last, Rose sincerely hoped, for at least another two years.

"I telephoned Jack," said Mrs. Runnall. "Meet him at Tottenham Court Road Tube Station and he'll take you out to lunch." The children received this in silence with glum faces. "Off you go, and try to look a bit pleased or you'll curdle the soup!" Laughing, she turned to the two assistants who had been hovering all the morning, "Children! There's no pleasing them! Whatever you arrange they want something else."

"Perhaps it's Mummy they want," said the elder of the two, who was in the habit of saying what she thought.

"Yes, well," said Hilda Runnall, giving herself an expert glance in the long mirror.

At the tube station they found Jack waiting, obliging as ever and just as boring. "Well, well, well," he said. "Here we are then. I expect you're both starving, so we'll just hop on a bus and I'll take you to a nice little place I know."

Jack was a big man, a little bit fat, and beginning to go bald, and with a large moustache. He had once been a major. He had never had children of his own and knew nothing about them, but in his view you couldn't go far wrong if you were hearty. So, he told himself, always be hearty, put them at their ease and, within reason, let them do exactly as they like. Consequently, Ricky and Rose had about as much respect for him as for their old teddy-bear.

"Still, it was a nice lunch he gave us," said Ricky as they trudged home across the common.

"What will you do with the money Mummy gave you?"

"Put it in my money-box."

"Meanie! Half of it was meant for me!"

"All right. You can have half of it. But perhaps I'll have to give it back."

"She'll never think of it again."

And that was true, oddly enough. Keen business woman though she was, where the children and the house were concerned Hilda Runnall was entirely careless about money. It therefore meant nothing to the children: they always had plenty, there was always plenty more where the last lot came from, so why should they worry? Mummy bought them everything they could possibly want, and a lot of things they didn't want, so they could spend their money, or save it, or give it away; even lose it—it didn't matter.

On the common there were many children and a number of care-free dogs. It was a lovely place (for London, that is) with grass and trees and plenty of space and no danger. It was not a park with flower-beds which you had to treat with respect, but just commonland for everyone's benefit. The big main road which cut through the centre of it, on which the traffic raced unceasingly all day, was too far away to matter. However hard you kicked a football it wouldn't go near it and so, when the weather was fine, all the balls came out—the footballs, the cricket balls, the tennis balls, the dogs' balls—and there was enough room for groups to play without getting in each other's way. Richard and Rose didn't belong to any of these groups. They could have done so perhaps if they had wanted to, or if they had been asked, but they didn't show any wish to join in so no one asked them. They went to different schools from most of the other children, their mothers didn't meet, and they hadn't lived in the district for long. London is a funny place. You can live and die in it without anyone taking the least bit of notice.

"I shall be glad when it's next week," said Rose.

"Going back to school, you mean. I thought you didn't like school."

"I don't really. Not much. Only it's better than doing nothing."

"There's plenty to do. The world's full of things to do. The only thing about school is they tell you when to do it. You don't always have to be making up your own mind."

"But you hate being told what to do."

"I don't mind at school. It's their job to push you around. Besides, at school there are people to do things with."

"You've got me to do things with at home."

"Oh, you, yes!"

"Well, anyway, what are you going to do now?"

"I'm going to finish my book and then go to the library."

"Yes, let's do that," agreed Rose. She also loved reading and their local library. It was modern and warm, with polished floors and armchairs and small tables, and, of course, shelves and shelves of books. The young lady in the children's department was nice too, and you could talk to her about books and she would help you to choose. If you were quiet you could stay there as long as you liked.

On their return from the library Richard rang the bell of the front door of their house. When Mrs. Mumford did not come, Rose banged the knocker and looked through the letter-box. "It's all quiet, Ricky. I don't think Mum's there."

"Let me look." Ricky put his eye to the letter-box. "No, you're right. She's not there. Funny how you can *see* when there's no one in a house."

"It isn't funny. If they were there you could see them."

"Silly! I mean, supposing Mum was in the kitchen. You can't see the kitchen from here but I know from the look of the house she isn't in the kitchen. You can *see* when a house is empty."

Rose gave it up. Frowning, she gave the bell another sharp ring but there was still no answer.

"But, Ricky, where is she? It's far too early for her to go yet. It's only ten past three."

"If she has gone she will have left the key under the mat. Yes, there it is. So she must have gone."

They went into the silent house. "Mum!" called Rose in a quavery voice at the foot of the stairs.

"She's left a note here on the kitchen table," called Richard. Scrawled on the pad of cheap paper, on which Mrs. Mumford used to write down her lists of wants and complaints, were six words: 'Sorry feeling bad I've gone home.'

Ricky and Rose looked at each other.

"Gawn," said Ricky, mimicking Mum. He expected Rose to laugh with him (they were both excellent mimics), but she didn't. She burst into tears.

"Oh, come off it, Rosie," said Ricky kindly. Rose almost never cried and why should she now? "There's nothing to cry about. She'll be back tomorrow."

But Rose went on crying, sniffing helplessly and wiping her eyes on the wide skirt of her pinky dress. She didn't know why she was crying and she was very much ashamed, but she could not stop.

"Tell you what," said Ricky. "You go on upstairs to our room and get on with your book, and I'll bring you up something. A surprise."

Still sniffing, Rose turned obediently and went upstairs. The children's bedrooms were on the top floor, but on the first floor they had a day-room of their own, which a generation or two back would have been called a nursery. Here they kept all their possessions, had their meals when Mr. and Mrs. Runnall were out, watched their own television set, read and played and quarrelled, and generally enjoyed themselves. It was a lovely large room and its wide windows looked out over the common, across to the main road which was so far away that the red London buses looked like toys.

Rose stood and looked out of the window. The trees

with their fresh green leaves were bowing gently in the wind, and the gulls were there, scores of them, as they often were during the winter months, snow-white against the grass, and there were pigeons strutting up and down, up and down, their heads jutting as they walked. She did not know why she had cried, or at least she could not have put it into words. She was not conscious of being particularly fond of Mum, but if Mum had to go—if she died, for instance—she felt as if her world would collapse. There had been many changes, two or three different houses before this one, then Daddy going, just going without saying a word—one day he was there and the next day he wasn't—then Jack coming and Mummy being out all day, and perhaps she mightn't come back either. you never knew. Mummy didn't often announce her plans in advance.

She heard Richard coming up the stairs and she sat down and took up a book, trying to look as if she were reading it. The surprise turned out to be an enamel tray with two glasses of a strange-coloured liquid, a box of chocolates, already opened, a tin of toffees, a box of dates and a round box of Turkish Delight still in its paper wrappings with a scarlet ribbon looped round it.

"Ooh, Ricky!" exclaimed Rose. It made her so happy when he was kind, and, though she really didn't want anything to eat, to please him she would have eaten the moon if he had taken the trouble to get it for her.

He put the tray carefully on the table by the window.

"Hullo," he said. "There's your old lady outside."

CHAPTER 3

In a flash, without thinking, Rose was down the stairs and out of the front door and across the road to where Mrs. Beewater and Chuffy were standing looking at each other.

"My dear!" said Mrs. Beewater, noting the stain of tears on Rose's face. But having got there Rose did not know what to say. She simply stood, her hands tightly clasped in front of her.

"I hope it's nothing serious?"

Rose swallowed. She said, "Not really. Mum's ill. She left a note to say she was feeling bad and gawn 'ome." Unconsciously Rose said it exactly as Mrs. Mumford would have said it.

"Your mother is ill? I am sorry."

"Not Mummy. Mum—Mrs. Mumford."

"I had forgotten you had two mothers," said Mrs. Beewater, half to herself. "Is Mummy at home?"

"No. She's at a board meeting."

"So you and your brother are all alone. Well, you'll catch cold standing here in that thin dress. How the wind does blow on this common! Come, let's go inside and see if there is anything to be done."

Richard, watching from the window upstairs, saw his sister and the old lady coming towards the house, he heard the door slam and then their footsteps on the stairs. Whatever is Rose playing at? he wondered. She was odd at times though usually quite sensible. Standing by the table with the drinks and the sweets he looked rather forbidding as the two entered the room. Rose knew this look well. So did Mrs. Beewater. She had seen it many times on the faces of her men-folk and she was well accustomed to handling tricky situations.

"Well, Richard, I am sorry to hear of Mrs. Mumford's illness," she began conversationally, as if to her grown-up son.

"I don't expect she's too bad," returned Ricky. "She was all right when we came in after lunch and I can't think why Rose is so upset about it. She's been away before."

Rose looked at the floor. She did not attempt to explain. Nobody would have understood. She only knew she felt desperate and lost as if she were alone in a dark forest.

"I am afraid I have interrupted a party," said Mrs. Beewater, looking at the two glasses and their curious contents.

"Won't you sit down?" said Ricky, hospitable at last. "Would you like a drink?"

"Er—I think not, thank you. You have only two glasses there. I'll have—dear me, what a tempting array. If you are opening that box of Turkish Delight—I'm very fond of it. Yes, I will sit down for just one minute."

The 'party' was soon in full swing, Richard and Rose sipping their drinks, Mrs. Beewater enjoying Turkish Delight.

"What *is* this, Ricky?" Rose asked after her second sip.

"Well, I told you I'd bring you a surprise and this was the only thing I could think of. It's a mixed drink, you see: lemon squash and some golden syrup and the juice from the tinned peaches we had yesterday, and soda water—oh, and a little ginger, and some of that grape-juice, and just to top it up a spoonful of Nescafé. Do you like it?" he demanded.

"It's *lovely*, Ricky. Specially when you get used to it."

"You would make a good cook, Richard," commented Mrs. Beewater.

"I like cooking. Mum often lets me do some, and my things always come out better than Rose's."

"They do not then!" retorted Rose.

Presently the conversation turned to supper and Mrs. Mumford. It was then about five o'clock. Mrs. Beewater's 'minute' had become unexpectedly prolonged in carefree and (to the three indulging in it) delightful conversation.

Usually, the children explained, Mum left everything ready and Mummy just finished things off when she came home. Jack usually came in earlier than she did but he wasn't much good at anything like that.

"But I don't know," said Rose, "if she will have left anything today. Did you notice, Ricky?"

Mrs. Beewater sat back in her chair and listened to the two children sorting things out.

Then Rose said, "D'you know, Ricky, I think we'd better phone Mummy. Last time Mum wasn't here she brought home a chicken all ready, and she won't like it if there's nothing to eat."

"I think that is a very good idea," said Mrs. Beewater. "Richard, you go and telephone, and, Rose, you and I will go and lay the table."

By this time Ricky and Rose felt they knew Mrs. Beewater so well that they jumped up joyfully to carry out her suggestion. In the dining-room Mrs. Beewater watched while Rose put out the table mats and the silver, lending a hand only as Rose gave the lead. When it was finished the two stood back to survey their work.

"The flowers could do with a little attention, don't you think?" said Mrs. Beewater. "Let's cut their tails and give them some fresh water. Well, Richard, what did your mother say?"

"She said, 'How tiresome!' You know, Rose, how she does."

"How tiresome!" mimicked Rose gleefully. "But what did she say about food? I'm awfully hungry."

"She said it was to be cold tonight anyway and there

should be a lettuce and what-not in the fridge, so we are to make a salad and find a tin of something in the larder, and she'll bring home an ice-cream block."

"Well, if it's all cold we'll start with a tin of soup," said Rose practically. "Come along, Mrs. Beewater, we must put out soup spoons and put the plates to heat."

"Give me something else to do too," said Mrs. Beewater.

"You can cut the cucumber and beetroot," said Richard, handing her a knife. "I'm sure you'll do it thinner than we shall. And, Rose, you had better grate a carrot."

By the time everything was ready it was nearly six o'clock. Mrs. Beewater blinked as she looked at her watch. It was a long time since she had enjoyed herself so much and the minutes had fled unnoticed. "When does your mother get home?" she asked guiltily.

"Usually about seven, but Jack will be in any time now."

Mrs. Beewater seized her short sealskin jacket which she had hung over the back of a chair and hastily struggled into it. "I must go at once. What will you do if Mrs. Mumford doesn't come tomorrow? Who will do everything?"

The children shrugged their shoulders. "Us probably. Or else no one will do it. Or Mummy will do it all on Saturday. It depends."

"Now listen," said Mrs. Beewater, pausing in the hall, "I have had an idea. I will come past your house tomorrow at half past nine. You, Rose, will watch for me and come out and tell me how the land lies. If Mrs. Mumford is here I shall just go on, but if she is not"—she laid a finger lightly on her lips—"I will come in and help you, and not a word to anyone. It's a secret between us three. Goodbye!"

Mrs. Mumford did not come for the rest of that week, and every day Mrs. Beewater, putting on a ridiculous little apron, assisted in hoovering, dusting, washing-up and bed-making. She knew very well she was taking an unwarrantable liberty, walking unasked, unknown even, into another woman's house, encouraging her children to keep her visits secret, but she did not greatly care. She was lonely and unhappy and sensed that Rose, at least, was lonely and unhappy too, and all her life Mrs. Beewater had been accustomed to doing exactly as she pleased. She did not, in fact, like housework and had never had to do it, but she was fascinated by Richard and Rose Anders. And Rose particularly, the grey-eyed, leggy Rose, had walked straight into her heart.

On the Saturday, Mrs. Runnall went round to Mrs. Mumford's house, demanding, "You're not leaving me, are you?"

"Everyone has a right to be ill sometimes," returned Mrs. Mumford. "I had gasteritis and artheritis and a good many other itises too, I shouldn't be surprised. Downright ill, I was."

"Well, I'm sorry," said Mrs. Runnall, "but when are you coming back?"

"I'll see how I feel Monday," said Mrs. Mumford, making no promises; but on Monday back she came and Mrs. Beewater's secret visits were inevitably over.

"You children have been quite wonderful," said Mrs. Runnall, who, if she did not often scold, did not often praise either. "You have worked so hard and everything is so spick and span you'd never know Mum had been away."

"I suggest we give Mum notice and let them carry on," said Jack, with a know-all wink at Ricky. "Save money all round. No school fees, no wages."

"I don't know about saving money," said Hilda, "because I absolutely must reward them. What would you like? Ricky? Rose?"

Ricky decided on money, but Rose, after much thought, said she would like a very large box of Turkish Delight.

"Whatever did you choose *that* for?" asked Ricky later. "There are always heaps of sweets in the larder and you can have them whenever you like."

"I wanted it for Mrs. Beewater," said Rose, hugging the box to her chest. "She did an awful lot, you know, and it wouldn't be fair for her not to have anything, and," she added, "I don't suppose we would have done much if she hadn't come in and encouraged us."

"That means you haven't got anything."

But Rose was indifferent. If she wanted anything she could always buy it.

"Why did she always say we mustn't ever tell anyone?"

"I don't think she ever said. I suppose she thought Mummy wouldn't like it. Well, they don't know each other, do they?"

The following afternoon Rose washed her face and combed her hair, wrapped the Turkish Delight in a piece of Christmas paper left over from the past year, and went to call on Mrs. Beewater. Jennifer and Marilyn came to the front door.

"Hullo," they said, their eyes wide. Rose had never been to see them before.

"Hullo," said Rose, staring back. Suddenly she felt shy, not of Jennifer and Marilyn, indeed not, but of a strange house and of Mrs. Steele whom she had seen and did not like, and of Mrs. Beewater who had not asked her to come.

"Is Mrs. Beewater in?"

"Granny? Yes."

"Can I see her, please."

Jennifer and Marilyn looked at each other uncertainly. How funny. Nobody ever came to see Granny except sometimes Uncle Gerard, and certainly not Rose Anders who didn't even know her. And Mummy, who always gave detailed instructions about everything, was out at a committee and had never told them what to do if someone unexpected called.

"I don't think you can," said Jennifer, the elder of the two. "She always has a rest in the afternoon."

"And Mummy's out," piped up Marilyn.

"Oh, well, in that case ..." said Rose, marching in. "Which is her bedroom, please?" She started walking upstairs, and the two little girls, realising the battle was lost, shut the front door hastily and ran up in front of her.

"There's someone to see you, Granny," said Jennifer breathlessly, at Mrs. Beewater's door.

"Who is it?" The voice sounded a little irritable.

"It's me," said Rose, squeezing past.

"I couldn't stop her coming," quavered Jennifer.

"I should think not indeed. She is never to be stopped. Do you hear me, Jennifer?"

"Yes, Granny."

The three children stood in the doorway uncertain what to do next, the two mousey little Steele girls gazing apprehensively at their grandmother, Rose Anders taller, thinner, straighter, looking interestedly round the room with its bay windows and handsome brocade curtains. Mrs. Beewater, a pale blue fluffy shawl round her shoulders, lay on her bed under the eiderdown comparing her grandchildren with this new, rather strange little friend.

"How nice of you to come and see me, Rose."

"Yes, well ..." She couldn't go on. How could she, with Jennifer and Marilyn standing there like stuffed dummies with their mouths open? She clutched her box tighter, and swallowed.

"Jennifer and Marilyn, go downstairs and get on with whatever you were doing. Rose has come to see me." And having dismissed her granddaughters, royally, as if they were ladies-in-waiting and she a queen, Mrs. Beewater plumped up her pillows, sat up a little higher, rearranged the fluffy blue cloud about her shoulders, and said kindly, "Dear Rose, I am so pleased to see you. Pull up that chair and sit beside me."

"I'm afraid I woke you up."

'No, no. Well, to be truthful, yes, you did. But no matter. I was having a not very pleasant dream."

"I have horrible dreams sometimes. What was it about?"

"I thought my husband was here and my son, and they were having an argument. They didn't always get on very well, you know. My son didn't approve of us."

"Didn't approve of you?"

"Well—it's hard to explain. My husband and I always had such a good time together. We saw eye to eye. We liked the same things."

"What sort of things?"

"Oh, exciting things. Camping in the desert. Going off on long treks, riding on elephants and camels, sailing boats—and spending money!"

"Do you mean your son didn't like those things?"

"He did when he was younger, but later on he grew, as I say, disapproving. Especially about money. He didn't think money was made to be spent, and my husband and I loved spending it. Well, when you came in—in my dream, I mean—my husband was saying to him, 'Gerard, I do wish you wouldn't speak to me as if you were my headmaster.' "

"Just as well I came then," commented Rose, laughing, "else they might have had a proper row."

"No. They never rowed. Gerard would never do anything so undignified." Mrs. Beewater smiled. "It's a funny thing, Rose. You have children, adorable little things, so helpless and weak and dependent on you for everything. And then suddenly you find they are big and grown-up and somehow rather frightening. And *you* are the weak one, dependent on *them*." She was not smiling now.

"Is—is Mrs. Steele disapproving too?"

Mrs. Beewater sighed for an answer. She could laugh at her son. He was only a man after all. But she could never laugh at her daughter, nor laugh with her either. This was her daughter's home, her daughter's furniture, her daughter's excellent taste. She was a stranger, a visitor in her daughter's house. None of this, of course, must be said to Rose, who went to school with her daughter's children. She pulled herself together.

"What have you got in that parcel, Rose?"

"It's for you."

"For me!" She undid the string and removed the beautiful Christmas paper. "Turkish Delight! Oh, Rose, how perfectly lovely. Such a beautiful box too."

"You said you liked Turkish Delight—you do like it, don't you?"

"I love it! Come, help me eat it." She offered the open box to Rose, but Rose held back, shaking her head.

"No. It's for you. It's a reward, you see, for helping me and Ricky with the housework."

Mrs. Beewater put the box down on the eiderdown and laughed and laughed. She looked about twenty years younger, and Rose thought she must have looked rather like that when she and her husband were doing exciting things spending their money.

"I must explain," Rose cried, her cheeks as pink as the Turkish Delight. "Just listen to me one minute. Mummy was so pleased because we had kept the house so nicely she said we could have whatever we liked, so I asked for this for you because really I don't think we should have done anything if you hadn't been there!"

"You didn't tell her about me, I hope!"

"Certainly not. It was our secret. I can't think why you didn't want her to know."

"Because I shouldn't have done it. One doesn't go uninvited into another woman's house." Then she added, "That was very sweet of you, Rose, but I assure you I didn't need any reward! It's a long time since I have enjoyed a week so much. Tell me, is Mrs. Mumford all right now? What was the matter with her?"

"I been ever so bad. Artheritis and gasteritis somethink crool," mimicked Rose. "Yes, she's all right now."

"I suppose it wouldn't be very kind to wish she would have it again."

"I suppose it wouldn't really." Rose crowed with delight at the memory. "But it was fun, wasn't it!"

CHAPTER 4

When Mrs. Steele came home from her committee, Rose had gone. The children met her in the hall and she greeted them in her usual cheery manner. "Well, my chickabiddies! Take these parcels, Marilyn; and, Jennifer, hang my coat up, on the hanger, neatly, mind you, and then you can both come and help me in the kitchen."

Mrs. Steele was a pretty woman with fluffy, honey-coloured hair and a fresh complexion. She was quite tall but comfortably rounded so that she did not look as tall as she really was. When you first saw her you thought, 'What a kind face; how sweet she is!' until you noticed that the sweetness of her face could become as hard and set as the sugar on a wedding-cake.

"What's this you're telling me?" she asked as she and Jennifer and Marilyn were all working busily in the kitchen. "Did you say that *Rose Anders* came to see *Granny* this afternoon? What did she come for?"

"She brought a parcel for her, and when I went up to Granny's room after Rose had gone I saw it open on the bed. It was Turkish Delight—and Granny was eating a piece!"

"Turkish De*light*!" exclaimed Margaret Steele, looking thoroughly wedding-cake-ish. "But why?"

"Granny sent us downstairs, so we don't know, and you wouldn't have liked us to listen at the door, would you?" finished Jennifer, virtuously.

"She said that Rose was to be allowed to see her whenever she liked," volunteered Marilyn.

"Well, that's enough of that," said Mrs. Steele briskly.

But if enough had been said by her daughters, Margaret Steele had made up her mind to say a good deal more herself on the subject of Rose Anders. Mrs. Beewater was prepared for it. She knew quite well that Jennifer and Marilyn would not have kept a still tongue in their heads and, after all, why should they?

"My dear Margaret, I really cannot at my age be told whom I am to be friendly with," she said when, later that evening, Mrs. Steele confronted her with her misdeeds.

"This is my house, Mother."

"I am well aware of that, Margaret."

"And you know I *particularly* told you that I did not wish my daughters to have anything to do with Rose Anders."

"So I sent your daughters out of the room the moment she arrived."

This was unanswerable. Margaret started on another tack. "But, Mother, it's so extra*ordinary* for you to have taken up with that child. And why should she bring *you* Turkish Delight?"

"Who says she did?" demanded Mrs. Beewater sharply, for the box had been hidden at the bottom of her wardrobe.

This again was unanswerable.

"It's no use arguing with her," Margaret told her husband when they were alone.

"Then don't argue with her," said Mr. Steele.

"What else can I *do*?"

"I don't really see why you should do anything."

"The child is quite—well, quite un-brought up. She might steal, she might do all sorts of undesirable things."

"Oh, come, Margaret! Your mother is no fool."

"I know she is a very wilful old lady!"

"You knew that before you invited her to come and live with us."

"Of course I did. But I had to ask her here. I couldn't leave her alone in that expensive flat with no money and the rent going up all the time, and no domestic help to be had. *And* Mother not eating properly."

"I know all that. You had to invite her, and I am not complaining, but you shouldn't be surprised to find she's difficult."

"I thought she'd settle *down!*" cried Margaret, with tears in her eyes. "I've given her everything. The best bedroom in the house, lovely food, clothes even—so I *do* think she owes it to me to do as I ask her!"

"Perhaps you had better put her in a home."

"*Robert!*" Appalled, Margaret faced her husband. "Put her in the *workhouse*, do you mean?"

"Don't be absurd, Margaret! There is no workhouse today."

"Well, an institution, I mean."

"No-o. There are homes which are quite nice. Watson put his mother into one. Quite satisfactory, he said it was."

"Robert, I couldn't! One doesn't put one's mother into a home."

"Doesn't one? Then one has to put up with her in one's own home."

So there for a time matters had to be left, but Mrs. Beewater knew that she was under a heavy cloud of disapproval from her daughter. This did not deter her, however, from seeing more of Rose, and Richard too if he happened to be about. She and Rose made opportunities to meet each other, sometimes in the warm and friendly library, occasionally in Mrs. Beewater's bedroom (though this was rather nerve-racking for them both) or in the children's own room when the grown-ups were safely out of the house, but more often just on the common with Chuffy keeping watch.

One afternoon in May, a Saturday when Mr. and Mrs. Steele had taken their little girls to a matinee, Rose spent quite a long time with Mrs. Beewater in her bedroom. Though it was certainly spring-time and the chestnut trees were in glorious green leaf, there was a penetrating east wind and Mrs. Beewater switched on her electric fire. The two of them sat in its warm glow, content and perfectly at ease.

"Tell me some more," said Rose, "about when you and your husband did exciting things together. No, I know! Begin at the beginning and tell me everything about when you were little."

"Suppose you tell me everything about you."

"There isn't anything to tell about me. Nothing's ever happened to me. But you are seventy-nine so there's been lots of time for things to happen to you. Tell me about when you were nine—or can't you remember such a long time ago?"

"Oh, yes, I can remember it," said Mrs. Beewater, staring at the fire, a little smile on her lips.

"When you were nine you must have been at school like me," prompted Rose.

"I never went to a school, except to a finishing school in Zurich."

"Never went to school? So didn't you ever learn anything?"

"We had governesses at home."

"Who's we?"

"My sister and I. My sister, Lilian. She was older than I, and much taller, so that I was always the little sister. And I had three brothers. They all went away to school, of course, very young, when they were about eight, but Lilian and I were both taught at home until we were old enough to go to Zurich."

"What did you learn at Zurich?"

"How to behave socially. How to dress. We had lessons in ballroom dancing, music, the arts, French and German, embroidery and other needlework. It was while I was at school in Zurich that my sister, Lilian, got married secretly, and I didn't see her again for years."

"Why? Why didn't you see her?"

"My father wouldn't let me. He didn't like her husband."

"Wasn't he a nice man?"

"I don't know. I expect he was. But I never saw him, you see. You won't understand, of course. He was a policeman and my father didn't think he was good enough for her."

"Why didn't he? I think policemen are *very* nice men."

"So they are. Usually. I'm sure Lilian's husband was or she wouldn't have married him—I suppose. But—well, as I said, you couldn't possibly understand, being a child of your time and not sixty years ago—my father was very proud of Lilian and he had spent a great deal of money on her. She was presented at Court, and he thought she ought to give him some return for it and make a good marriage, you understand. Instead she married a policeman, who, however good he was, was not particularly well educated; they weren't in those days."

"But still—if she liked him very much . . ."

"She did. She was terribly in love with him. She used to meet him in the shrubbery after dark. No one knew but me."

"Did she always love him?" asked Rose, well aware that marriages did not necessarily last for ever.

"I don't know. I suppose they were happy in their pokey little house. Then he was murdered."

"Oh!" cried Rose, her eyes popping out of her head.

"Yes. After they had been married about ten years. A gang set on him one dark night when he was out on his beat. It was in all the papers. My mother and father were terribly upset, more by the publicity than anything else, I'm afraid."

"Did she live at home after that?"

"Oh, no. She went on living in her little house with her two children, and she went out to work, I believe. But by that time I was married and away."

"But you did see her again, you said."

"Only once. In my cousin's house."

"And"—Rose had to think how to put this next burning question—"when you saw her—what was she like? Did you know her?"

"I knew her, of course. She looked very much the same. Tall, rather handsome, just as I'd remembered her—to look at, that is. But she herself was different. Life had changed so much for both of us, and I think she was angry with me because I hadn't disobeyed my father and got in touch with her. She didn't understand."

"I think your father was beastly. I shall marry whoever I want to!"

Mrs. Beewater looked at the serious little face with its grey eyes and up-lifted chin, and tried to see into the future. "I expect you will, Rose." "You have to remember," she said after a silence, "that my father belonged to his day just as you belong to yours. Thing were so different then; I can't tell you how different they were! Children expected to obey their parents and even when we were quite grown up we still did what they expected of us."

"Lilian didn't."

"And she had to take the consequences."

"Is Lilian still alive?"

"No. She died some years ago."

For a little time they sat in silence, the old lady remembering, the child imagining the tall girl, Lilian, who had married a policeman. Then Rose asked, "Are your brothers still alive?"

"No, they are all dead," returned Mrs. Beewater sadly. "At least, one may still be alive. He was the black sheep of the family; he never did anything—just wandered about the face of the earth. He was my favourite brother. Robin."

Rose thought again. She thought, Will Ricky and I be like that when we get old? Will we just never see each other? We shall marry and we shall die, of course—one day. "Why did Robin wander about the face of the earth?"

"Well—it's a long story. My father said he stole some money. So there was trouble and he left home."

"Did he steal it?"

"Possibly," said Mrs. Beewater after a pause. She fell into deep thought and seemed so far away that Rose did not like to disturb her with further questions, though there was a great deal more she wanted to know. Lilian must have had children, the brothers too, and they must all be old by this time. Why didn't Mrs. Beewater know them? It was obvious that she was not very happy in her daughter's house; why then didn't she go and live with a niece or a nephew? And Robin? He must be a very old man, older than Mrs. Beewater, and surely had had enough of wandering about the face of the earth. Why couldn't he and Mrs. Beewater meet and settle down together in a little house in Kensington where she so wanted to be?

She looked at the little gold clock with its glass sides, standing on the mantelpiece. Mummy and Jack were taking them out this evening.

"Goodbye," she said abruptly, jumping up.

"Yes, you had better go," agreed Mrs. Beewater, nodding at the little travelling clock which had accompanied her and her husband on so many of their travels. "When shall I see you again?"

Rose, dressed as usual in slim-fitting jeans, stood on one leg, one foot tucked behind a knee, a characteristic position for her when she was thinking.

"I don't know. Soon perhaps. It all depends."

She ran off and let herself quietly and rather guiltily out of the front door, her head full of excited sadness. Excited because Mrs. Beewater had been giving her glimpses of a far-off, different world; sad because she could feel Mrs. Beewater's sadness, and thought that one day it might be her own. There were no answers to her questions about herself and Ricky. Perhaps he too would wander, and she herself would have to live with a daughter she didn't particularly like, when she was seventy-nine. But that was impossible! Rose Anders would never be old! She ran and skipped all the way home.

CHAPTER 5

It was a quarter to five on a grey afternoon. Rose, having come home from school, had nothing to do. She stood at the window looking over the common towards the big main road where the toy-like traffic was still bowling along, fast and soundless. The trees were in full leaf, the grass was very green.

Mum has gone home, Mummy wouldn't be back for another two hours, Jack might be home at six but he scarcely counted, and Richard had gone off by himself. He was in one of his moods: he wouldn't talk, he merely jerked his shoulder in an impatient sort of way when Rose spoke to him, and then he had gone off, out of the house, by himself. When Rose ran after him calling, "Ricky, Ricky, can't I come too?" he had scowled and stumped off with his hands in his pockets. He was like that sometimes.

Rose was not a child who made friends easily. Her one real friend of her own age lived some way off and they rarely met except at school. On occasions they visited each other's home but this had to be by arrangement. The two little Steele girls were the ones who lived nearest but they could not by any stretch of imagination be called friends. Indeed Rose thought they avoided her and always looked the other way when they saw her coming— not that she cared. They had nothing in common, and Ricky could not bear the sight of them. It was odd that Mrs. Beewater should have granddaughters like that.

There was no hope of seeing Mrs. Beewater. Mrs. Steele would be in the house and Mrs. Beewater had a slight cold and was staying indoors.

Presently Rose too left the house, leaving the key under the doormat in case Richard should return home before she did. She rather hoped he would so that he also would feel alone and wonder where she was. Aimlessly she struck off across the common calling to Chuffy as she went, inviting him to take a walk with her, but beyond a slight twitch at the end of his tail he took no notice of her. He was too preoccupied watching and waiting. Rose thought she might go and see Mum, who would perhaps give her a cup of tea in her clean, dark, cosy little kitchen. Mum lived rather a long way off, but if a bus came it would be all right.

As Rose approached the main road she saw that something must have happened. At first she had thought that it was merely a traffic jam, but it was more than that. A bus had stopped on the near side so that she could not see, but it looked as if there had been an accident. What a bit of luck, thought Rose gratefully; she would be able to tell Ricky about it.

The bus moved slowly away, all its passengers craning their necks to see what was going on, and Rose could see a motorbike lying on its side and someone lying in the road and a man kneeling down doing things, and people standing round, heads bent, just watching. Then a white ambulance, its siren shrieking, rushed towards the knot of people who scattered hastily as it drew up beside the curb. Cars on both sides of the road were slowing up, partly for safety, partly out of curiosity, so Rose was able to cross quite easily.

The doors of the ambulance were open, the men were carrying a stretcher with a figure on it covered with a rug. Being small, Rose was able to dodge between the people and push her way to the front. With fearful fascination she let her eyes travel along the still form under the rug to the white face on the pillow.

It was Ricky's white face. Eyes shut. A great purple

lump on his cheek. Blood on his forehead.

She was paralysed with shock. She wanted to cry out, to speak to him, but the words would not leave her throat.

"Out of the way, missy," said one of the men briskly. Then the doors of the ambulance were shut—with Ricky inside—the awful blue glass hiding everything.

"It's my brother!" she cried. But no one heard her, and who was going to notice a small girl among a crowd of people who had something far more interesting to look at?

"That was my brother!" she said again as the ambulance moved gently away.

"Eh? What's that?" said a man staring at her.

"My brother," repeated Rose desperately. "Where are they taking him?"

"You'd better come and talk to this young gentleman," said the man, taking her arm and steering her through the crowd to a pasty-faced lad standing shakily by the overturned motorbike. Rose recognised him; his name was Len.

"Hullo, Rose," Len croaked, trying to smile, and at that moment a police car drove up and two policemen got out and made straight for him. Rose edged away. "Where are they taking him?" she asked the man who had led her to Len.

"St. Peter's, I wouldn't be surprised, seeing the ambulance has headed that way. Did you see what happened?"

Rose shook her head. Her legs, which had brought her so easily across the common a minute or two before, now seemed too weak to move. It was an effort to lift her feet but she shook herself into action and left the crowds behind her. She crossed the road and began to run with only one thought in her head: Mrs. Beewater. Never mind if Mrs. Steele was there, never mind if she was cross. Mrs. Beewater was her friend and a friend was what she needed.

Mrs. Steele herself came to the door accompanied by a

lovely smell of cooking, Jennifer and Marilyn peeping from behind her.

"Well?" said Mrs. Steele, then, her tone changing, "My dear! What *is* the matter?"

"Mrs. Beewater," mumbled Rose, her eyes enormous.

"Mother!" Mrs. Steele called sharply over her shoulder. "Come in, Rose!" She took hold of Rose firmly, drew her inside and shut the front door. "There seems to be some trouble here," she said as Mrs. Beewater came slowly down the stairs.

"Rose," said Mrs. Beewater kindly and the tears began to stream down Rose's face though she made no sound.

"Accident," she gasped at length. "Ricky. They took him away in an ambulance."

"Is he badly hurt?"

Rose shook her head. "I don't know—didn't see what happened." Tears choked her.

Mrs. Steele became very kind. She made Rose a cup of very hot tea, she discovered which hospital Richard was in, she telephoned Hilda Runnall, she got the car out, gave precise instructions to her mother and daughters, and whisked Rose off to St. Peter's hospital, all within the space of fifteen minutes.

"They say there is nothing to worry about," she informed Rose as she drove expertly through the rush-hour traffic. "Probably just concussion and a broken arm."

"I thought he was dead," said Rose. "He looked dead."

"Not dead, no," said Mrs. Steele cheerfully. "Anyway, dear, I can't tell you how glad I am you came to us."

She was being so kind, Rose hadn't the heart to tell her that it was Mrs. Beewater she had run to and no one else.

At the hospital, after long enquiries at the information desk, they were sent to a small waiting room with white walls and pretty curtains and several small armchairs. Here they waited again, and presently Rose's mother was shown in, looking very handsome and tall and well-dressed, and, Rose noticed, perfectly at ease, in spite of the fact that her son had just met with an accident. Rose thought uncomfortably of her own face, swollen and streaked with tears, and a bit dirty too; she had caught sight of it quite by accident in a mirror.

All three talked things over for a time, then Hilda Runnall said, "You have been most kind, Mrs. Steele. I don't know what we should have done without you, but I don't think I ought to let you wait any longer. I can carry on from here."

"Well——" said Margaret Steele uncertainly. She looked at Rose. "I am so glad to have been able to help. The poor child was in such a state. You will let me know if I can do anything further?"

"I will indeed," said Hilda Runnall.

Directly Mrs. Steele had gone, Hilda turned to Rose without her professional smile. "However did that woman get in on this?" But before Rose could answer, and much to her relief (as she realised that her mother knew nothing at all about Mrs. Beewater and she couldn't at that moment have explained, she was feeling so funny inside), a young man in a white coat came in. He was the Casualty doctor.

"Mrs. Anders?" (Mrs. Steele had given particulars of Richard over the telephone.)

"I am Richard's mother, yes."

"I am admitting him to hospital. He is rather badly concussed, and his right arm is fractured."

"There is nothing very serious?" asked Mrs. Runnall, her face wrinkled into a frown.

"As far as we can tell at present, no."

"May I see him?"

"Me too?" put in Rose anxiously.

"They are just getting him into bed. But Sister will want to see you anyway, if you will wait a few minutes. What happened, d'you know?"

They both looked at Rose. "I wasn't there. He went off

without me. On a motorbike, I think—with Len," she explained at her mother's startled exclamation.

The young doctor smiled at Rose. "See what happens when you let your brother off the lead! Well, you won't have to worry for a little while. We'll keep him safe for you."

After what seemed a very long time they were allowed to leave the little waiting room, and go upstairs and along a corridor to the ward. The Sister asked a great many questions and wrote the answers down on a form. Then she allowed them to have a brief peep at Richard, neatly tucked up in bed, the curtains still drawn around him. He was unconscious and there was a bandage round his head. He looked so small, so defenceless, that Rose thought she was going to cry again, but fortunately they stayed only a minute or two; there was nothing to stay for.

They drove home in silence. Supper was barely finished when the police arrived, two of them, looking very smart and handsome in their uniform, so that Rose was immediately reminded of Mrs. Beewater's sister, Lilian. For the first time they heard the cause of the accident. The boy, Len, had borrowed his brother's motor-cycle. He had very often ridden it but had no licence. He was not a bad boy but he was frequently in and out of jobs and was then not working. He was alone and bored and could not resist showing off, and Richard Anders was also alone and bored and very willing to go pillion-riding. They had been several miles, Len had told the police, and were on their way home at a fairly good pace when the car in front braked sharply, Len had swerved, and Richard, who, Len thought, had been sitting with his hands in his pockets, had been thrown off. And that was all there was to it, the policemen said.

"So there we are," said Jack Runnall, after showing the policemen out. "Could have been worse, I suppose."

"You still have not explained," said Mrs. Runnall,

looking hard at Rose, "how you came to go to Mrs. Steele for help."

Rose said, "I didn't really. I went to Mrs. Beewater."

"And who is she?"

"Jennifer and Marilyn's granny. I go to school with them." Rose thought this would sound better somehow, more understandable.

"Let me get this straight. Jennifer and Marilyn are—who are they?—Mrs. Steele's daughters—right? So this Mrs. Funny-Name—Beewater?—is Mrs. Steele's mother. I see. No, Rose, I *don't* see. Are these two girls friends of yours?"

"No."

"Then for Pete's sake! How come?"

"I just like her, that's all."

"How did you get to know her?"

Rose shrugged.

"Understand me, Rose. It's very rarely I put my foot down where you and Ricky are concerned. But this time I'm going to. I do not wish you to have anything to do with the Steele family, grandmother, mother or children. Is that clear?"

"But Mrs. Steele was very kind, Mummy," said Rose, looking stubborn. "I don't like her, but she was kind."

Hilda Runnall laughed. "Kind, yes. Margaret Steele is always kind when she's putting the world to rights. 'My finger in every pie'—that's her motto. The Great Do-Gooder!" She switched her attention from Rose to Jack. "Do you know, she told me my children were neglected and that I ought to give up my business to look after them!"

Jack glanced at Rose and back at his wife with a 'not-in-front-of-the-children' look, but Hilda went on, not angrily, not bitterly, just talking: "If you could see those two little girls of hers! A little neglect is what they need. Like two little pots of chicken and ham paste. Not a spark of life in them." She stood up. "Now, Rose, up to bed, darling; you look tired out. Have a nice warm bath, and when you're in bed I'll send Jack up with an aspirin and some hot milk."

And so with Richard in hospital Rose was even more at a loose end when she was not at school. Two or three times a week she went with Mummy or Jack to visit Ricky, and quite often Mum was very kind in letting her go to her house for a cup of tea after school. Occasionally she went to the homes of school friends, but there were not many she could be bothered with and they all lived some way off. Sometimes she would go to the library and there, by chance or by arrangement, she would meet Mrs. Beewater.

Mrs. Beewater read a great deal and she was always interested in what Rose was reading or had read. "I wouldn't waste your time with that," she would say. "You want to read books which will teach you something, not only keep you amused. You know what they say? 'Never read a good book, only read the best.'"

Rose often wondered how she had managed to live before Mrs. Beewater came on the scene.

Since Richard's accident Mrs. Steele too had been more friendly because she had now got it fixed firmly in her head that of all the people living round this large London common Rose had rushed straight to her when she was in trouble. Rose had not told her, or Mrs. Beewater, of her mother's injunction to have nothing to do with 'grandmother, mother or children', for something warned her, quite correctly, that the grown-ups' code would insist on her respecting her mother's wishes. So, now that Mrs. Steele was less formidable, Rose went sometimes, not too often, to the house and straight up to Mrs. Beewater's room where she was always sure of a welcome. "After all," she used to argue with herself, "even if Mummy said I wasn't to see her, I didn't promise I wouldn't!"

It happened that one afternoon she arrived when Mrs. Beewater was turning out her books, of which she had many. There were piles on the floor and on the bed.

"Just the person I want," cried Mrs. Beewater. "You can help me to put all these back. Here's a duster. I've cleaned out that bookcase, so perhaps you will dust the books and put them back. Open them first and give them a good slap together—see, like this."

Rose loved being told what to do, or rather she loved doing things with other people, older people if she liked them. Happily she set to work.

The books were lovely, in good condition, well-bound, in reds and greens and blues, with gold or silver lettering on their backs. Some still had colourful dust-jackets. Rose stroked them gently as she put them in their places. The very old books with dull leather covers were in a book-case by themselves and Mrs. Beewater was dealing with these herself, dusting each one with affection and care.

The two talked as they worked, but presently Mrs. Beewater became aware of a deep silence, and she turned to look at Rose, who had come to a full stop, lost in a black leather-bound book, very large and heavy.

CHAPTER 6

For a few minutes Mrs. Beewater watched, saying nothing. The child was on her knees, leaning on her elbows, her shabby sandals sticking out behind her, and her yellow hair all over her face. The book was open before her on the faded Persian carpet. Utterly absorbed she was turning over the leaves and studying its many coloured pictures.

"What have you got there?" asked Mrs. Beewater at length, unable to contain her curiosity.

Rose looked up through her hair. "It's a Bible. And it has pictures. Look—look at this one." She scrambled to her feet, the book open in her hands.

"Show me," said Mrs. Beewater, sitting down in her armchair and pulling up a stool for Rose.

They bent over the picture. It was by Harold Copping, in colour. It depicted a group of men in Eastern robes, some sitting, some standing round a man seated on some stone steps, a little boy on his knee. Above them, a few steps higher up, another little boy sat, leaning against the wall, listening intently and watching all that was going on; indeed everyone was watching and listening as the man talked to them and the little boy perched on his knee. The man's arm was round the child, who was sitting, relaxed and comfortable, and not the least bit afraid.

Rose read the caption underneath the picture: *The Little Child Set in the Midst.* "In the midst of *what*?" she asked.

Mrs. Beewater looked closer. "There's a reference. I

can't see it. What does it say, Rose?"

"Matthew 18, 1 to 7." And Mrs. Beewater turned back a page and read the third verse: " 'I say unto you, Except ye be converted, and become as little children, ye shall not enter into the kingdom of heaven.' "

"What does it mean?"

Mrs. Beewater considered. It was a long time since she had thought about such things. She said, "We had better read the whole story," and she read: " 'The disciples came unto Jesus, saying, Who is the greatest in the kingdom of heaven? And Jesus called a little child unto him, and set him in the midst of them . . .' "

"So the man sitting on the steps is Jesus. Of course, I knew it was. Who is the little boy?"

"It doesn't say. Just a child who happened to be standing about, I expect. You know how little boys do stand and watch when anything is going on."

"He looks very comfortable with the man's arm round him. He doesn't look as if he wants to get down, does he?"

"He wouldn't want to get down. Jesus loved children, you see. He said, 'Let the little children come unto me', and He took them up in His arms and blessed them."

"What does 'bless' mean? How did He do it?"

"I don't know," said Mrs. Beewater helplessly. "I never did know what it meant. He prayed for them, I suppose."

"Look, there's another picture of Him with a child in His arms." Rose rustled the pages over quickly. "There. He's standing up with women round Him this time and a child in His arms. I think she's a girl, and she's holding on to His robe, look. Mark 10, 13 to 16. Go on, read it."

" 'They brought young children to Him, that He should touch them: and His disciples rebuked those that brought them. But when Jesus saw it, He was much displeased, and said unto them, Suffer the little children to come unto me, and forbid them not: for of such is the kingdom of God ... and He took them up in His arms, put His hands upon them, and blessed them.' "

"What you said," commented Rose. "It seems to me," she said slowly, "that Jesus thought the little ones were extremely important."

They examined many of the other pictures, all by Harold Copping. There was one which both Rose and Mrs. Beewater found specially lovely, entitled: *The Lost Piece of Silver,* of a woman very beautiful in her Eastern robes which glowed purple and red in the light of a tiny oil lamp, a look of great joy on her face as she gazed at a shining piece of silver in the palm of her hand. Rose read the reference herself, from the 15th chapter of Luke: " 'What woman having ten pieces of silver, if she lose one piece, doth not light a candle, and sweep the house, and seek diligently till she find it? And when she hath found it, she calleth her friends and her neighbours together, saying, Rejoice with me; for I have found the piece which I had lost. Likewise, I say unto you, there is joy in the presence of the angels of God over one sinner that repenteth.' "

When Rose had gone, Mrs. Beewater sat for some time lost in thought. Was it she herself, Helena Beewater, who had been saying such things to a child? Out of what far distant life, what dim corner of her mind, had those truths (were they truths?) come? They had not entered her conscious thoughts for more years than she liked to remember, and yet, without a moment's warning, they had jumped right back into place. 'Suffer the little children to come unto me, and forbid them not ...' Who was it who used to quote those words to her? Not her mother; certainly not her mother! Nanny? A governess? In a long succession of these estimable women not one had ever said such things to her, as far as she could remember, though they had all accompanied her to church with monotonous regularity. No, it was the housemaid they had had 'at home' for years. Minnie! Minnie Brown? No,

Barnes. That was her name: Minnie Barnes!

This Minnie used to look after her on Nanny's day out, and Lilian too if she was around. Minnie used to take them for walks when the weather was fine, and in the winter they would sit by the fire and talk. Minnie was always kind. (Oh, for a Minnie to look after me now, yes, and to love me, thought Mrs. Beewater fiercely, because Minnie *did* love me, I know, although I don't think I was ever very nice to her. I took it all for granted! She used to read Bible stories to me and once she gave me a text, rather crudely coloured. It said, Rest in the Lord, and I liked it and hung it on the wall; then Nanny saw it and tore it down and threw it in the waste-paper basket. Minnie must have seen it when she turned out the room the next day. Poor Minnie, did she mind? Happy Minnie! She was always happy. She rested in the Lord—was that the reason?)

Impatiently Mrs. Beewater got up and walked about the room. What is the matter with me? she thought angrily. Why should a child be able to stir me so much? It's absurd!

Then, still impatiently, but with curiosity, she took up the big Bible again still lying open at the picture of *The Little Child Set in the Midst*. She examined it closely, thinking of Rose. Why had she been so fascinated by it? It was not by any means one of the most interesting, or exciting, or beautiful of the pictures, but it was to that one she returned several times, poring over it and taking a keen interest in its every detail.

"Look at the little boy sitting alone," she had said; "he's listening very hard, but why doesn't he come nearer? If he came down two or three steps he would be right beside the man with the other little boy on His knee instead of being right outside. Do you think Jesus knew he was there? If He did, why didn't He tell him to come nearer so that He could put His arm round him too? Is it a true story, Mrs. Beewater?"

And what had she replied? She didn't know. Was it a true story? Certainly Minnie had believed it to be true; she had believed with all her heart that the Bible was the Word of God. How simple it would be, thought Mrs. Beewater, if I had a faith like Minnie's!

She thought then that she understood Rose's interest in the picture. To her it represented security. The child looked so safe, and so content with that arm around him, so comfortable sitting on the knee of a man who was both strong and kind. And Rose, no doubt, did not feel secure, the world she had known having been torn apart by divorce, her father now in America and her mother always away at work and too busy to be a proper mother.

Don't we all want security? thought Mrs. Beewater. Don't we all want someone to love us and look after us? A few minutes back she had longed for Minnie Barnes, but Minnie, that good, kind girl, had vanished in the mist of years and she would never come again. My insecurity is far greater than Rose's, she thought; she has her youth and all her life in front of her. I have nothing but old age. Nothing, nothing.

Sitting down, the big Bible in her lap, she began to read.

CHAPTER 7

All through that cold and windy summer, while Rose was at school and Richard was recovering from his accident, Mrs. Steele was very busy visiting homes for old people. First she discussed things with a social worker who gave her a list of addresses, and then she sat in her bedroom, the door fast shut, telephoning in a low voice. Hours she spent on the telephone because Margaret Steele was nothing if not thorough, and then off she would go in the car telling nobody anything before she went and discussing nothing after her return. But on the way home she would discuss things with herself, explaining, explaining away, arguing, trying to convince herself.

"It's not as if she were happy with us," she would say, not quite out loud. "We have done our best with her but she doesn't appreciate it; she only wants to get back to Kensington. No, I can't find a suitable place for her in Kensington; all too frightfully expensive and we should have to foot the bill (if only they'd *saved* something when Father had all those thousands a year!). The trouble is she wouldn't share a room—well, I couldn't ask her to really, but there is it: you can't find a single room in that sort of home and if you do it's too hideously expensive." And so, muttering to herself, she would drive grimly home and sit through the evening, her lips pressed tightly together.

Mrs. Beewater did not worry overmuch. She knew her Margaret, or so she thought, and it was evident she had something on her mind—something to do with herself, Mrs. Beewater had no doubt, but she felt herself more

than a match for her daughter. They had never got on
and they never would. It was awkward, of course, when
they were living together. But I shan't live for ever, she
told herself comfortably, though she didn't really believe
that: like most people who have always been the centre
of their own world she could not imagine that world
without her—until, in moments of truth, she had to realise that her world existed no longer, and she was left,
adrift, with no place of her own.

"Rose," she said one day, "do you think you could call
me Helena?"

"Helena," Rose repeated, frowning. "Why?"

"It is my name. And, do you know, there is no one in
the whole world to call me by it now. All my own generation has gone. Dead."

Rose thought about this. "What was your other name?
Before you married, I mean."

"Carlingshaw."

"Helena Carlingshaw. Helena Beewater." She rolled
the names on her tongue with her eyes shut, trying to see
the girl, Helena, and her tall sister Lilian, who had married the policeman; the favourite brother, Robin, who
had wandered about the face of the earth. Carlingshaw—
Carlingshaw—the fierce old father who had cut his
daughter out of his life. She opened her eyes and shut
them again to go on exploring those far off paths. Helena
Beewater. The sort of name that lovely exciting things
happened to: a husband who made roads in the jungle
and took you riding on camels and camping in the desert.

She opened her eyes and fixed the upright, smartly
dressed old lady with a long stare, then said slowly, "I
shall find it very difficult at first, but I will if you want me
to—call you Helena."

"I do want you to," said Mrs. Beewater.

Oddly enough it was that which brought matters to a
head. A little while after that conversation, Margaret
Steele said, "Mother, did I really hear that child, Rose

Anders, calling you by your Christian name?"

"Quite possibly," said Mrs. Beewater equably.

"But—do you *let* her?"

"I asked her to call me Helena."

"But how extraordinary! I mean, even I would never call you that."

"I should think not! That would be a very different matter."

"I can't under*stand* you." They were drinking coffee after dinner. The evening was chilly and Margaret had lit a log fire. Now she put down her cup with a bang and waved a hand. "Your own grandaughters—this Rose Anders apparently means *much* more to you than they do!"

Mrs. Beewater did not answer at once. Then she looked at her daughter and said quietly, "I have told you before, Margaret, that I must be allowed to choose my own friends. Furthermore, Jennifer and Marilyn are your daughters, not my granddaughters."

"What on *earth* can you mean by *that*?"

"They have never been allowed to be my grandchildren. If they came to see me at the flat in Kensington you were always with them, you answered for them, they had to sit still in their best dresses. I scarcely knew they were alive. Now they are older they are completely dominated by you; your pale little shadows. You smother them."

Robert Steele stood up. "You have said more than enough!"

Mrs. Beewater also stood up. "I have finished," she said, and turned to go.

"But I have *not* finished," said Margaret, also standing, with her back against the door. Her eyes were two blue glints of light in her sweet, hard face. "What you say about my children may well be true. Maybe I have gone too much the other way. I was determined that *my* daughters should belong to me and I to them, and that I would give them all the time I could. I was never your daughter. You never had time for me ..."

Mrs. Beewater gasped, but Margaret went relentlessly on, the bitterness of years welling up and breaking forth. "... nor for Gerard either. We didn't count. Father was your life. Your interests and his were all that mattered. You paid people to look after us. You sent us away to school—that's why *my* daughters will never be sent to boarding school—and when you were abroad we didn't see you for months, sometimes years——"

"My place was with my husband," said Mrs. Beewater, trembling, but still with dignity. "You cannot blame me for going with him when his work took him abroad. He needed me."

"Oh, yes, he needed you! Never was a man more fond of being looked after and cosseted. He had you exactly where he wanted you. But didn't *we* need you?" Margaret was crying now, the tears streaming down her face. "People shouldn't *have* children if they aren't going to love them and care for them."

"Margaret! I did love you and care for you!"

"You provided everything for us. There was no lack of money and you knew what was what. But we had no love. Perhaps I do smother my children, as you so kindly put it; but at *least* they have a mother, which is more than I *ever* had."

Robert Steele, acutely embarrassed, looked from one woman to the other. He had known for years that his wife had felt this way about her bringing up, but it was quite obvious to him that his poor mother-in-law had had no idea of the depth of bitterness her daughter had been storing up against her. And what was done was done; it was no use raking up the past. "Margaret," he said helplessly, taking her arm, and eventually she allowed him to lead her away from the door.

Mrs. Beewater went up to her room.

When at last she could bring herself to go to bed she tossed about most of the night unable to sleep. Was it true what her daughter had said? Had she failed her children? Was the popular saying true: that a woman is either a wife or a mother, never both? Certainly her husband had had first place in her life, and nothing was important unless he was the centre of it.

"Oh, my dear, my dear one," she cried in her heart, hugging herself in her arms and rocking backwards and forwards, "I loved you so. Why do I have to go on living without you?"

In the morning while Mrs. Beewater was having her first cup of tea, Mrs. Steele came in and stood at the end of the bed. She looked kind. But determined.

"Mother," she began, "we have to speak plainly."

"More plainly than we did last night," said Mrs. Beewater, smiling.

"We both said things we did not mean—or, at least, things we should not have said. But we must be realistic. You have been with us nine months."

"Ten next week."

"Ten then. And you are not happy."

"No."

"How can we *make* you happy?"

"I want to go back to Kensington."

"You know you *can't*!"

"I know I can't. Therefore I am not happy." She rearranged her bed-jacket, then looked squarely at her daughter. "As you pointed out so plainly last night, I lived for my husband. Now he is gone and there is no purpose in life."

"It's all very well *saying* that——"

"I know. I have to go on living. But don't blame me for not being happy."

"I do rather blame you. You have everything we can give you: this nice room—it *is* a nice room, isn't it?"

"Very nice. In perfect taste, dear."

"We try to be kind to you."

Mrs. Beewater snorted with disgust. *Try to be kind to*

you. Was she the kind of person to whom people had to try to be kind? Now she knew what old age really meant!

"Mother——" Desperately Margaret Steele sought for words which would convey her meaning without being hurtful. "We, Robert and I, have been talking things over and we think, perhaps, you shouldn't *stay* here any longer. You might be happier elsewhere."

"Where?" Mrs. Beewater's eyes searched her daughter's face for any hint of the fate that was being prepared for her.

"Well—you see—I've been looking at several places..."

"What sort of places!"

"Oh, very nice places—well, some of them were nicer than others," said Margaret, speaking very rapidly, "and it goes without saying that we shouldn't *want* you to go anywhere that *wasn't* nice, and this place does seem ... It's pleasantly furnished; single rooms, of course—nice garden—trees, you know..."

Mrs. Beewater, gazing at her daughter with frozen intensity, interrupted with, "Margaret! What place?"

"It's called The Homestead."

"A home for old people?"

"Yes, well, you could call it that. It's a woman—Mrs. Jenkins her name is—rather nice, I thought, and she takes in three or four old—well, you know—*elderly* people. She has one man, a nice old gentleman, so it isn't only women, which is rather nicer, I thought..."

"Please refrain from using the word *nice* again," said Mrs. Beewater, her voice colder than ice. "What could be nice about an old people's home? Margaret, I will not go! You can't just put me away as if I were an old dog (it would be easier no doubt if you could!). I will be consulted before you 'put' me anywhere!"

"Of course, Mother. You must see the place for yourself. I will take you there and you'll see how n ... I mean, *obviously* you must see it before you make up your mind, but you'll like it—I know you will." Her voice tailed off uncertainly. Mrs. Beewater's eyes, black with feeling, were un-nerving her. This, she thought, was the worst moment of her life.

"I will not go. Not even to see it. I refuse to go to any home however 'nice'. You can't do this to me. I will consult Gerard at once."

"Gerard knows."

"And he—agrees?"

"He sees there is nothing else to do." Margaret turned and left the room, shutting the door very quietly behind her.

For several minutes her mother sat perfectly still, staring at the fleecy green blanket on her bed. I'm trapped, she thought. Something broke within her, and she began to cry quietly, bitterly, with deep, painful sobs. God help me, she cried silently. Only He can! But why should He? I don't know Him; I've never had anything to do with God since I was a child, not since the days of Minnie Barnes. All the same, help me, help me!

The next few days the two women avoided each other as much as possible, each oppressed with frustration and bitterness. Mrs. Beewater, at her own request, had all her meals up in her room. Robert Steele felt quite unable to cope with the situation, especially when Margaret pleaded with him to 'say something' to her mother. "What can I say, Margaret? You have decided she is to go to a home. There is no point in discussing it further."

Margaret closed her eyes wearily. "I didn't decide it by myself. You suggested it in the first place. Yes, you did: you said that Watson put his mother in a home and it was quite nice."

"I merely put it forward as an alternative. *I* don't want her to go. It's for your sake entirely."

"Oh, of *course*. Why don't you say at once that I am an unfeeling wretch! You see her for about an hour a day in the evening—when you're at home. I have her all the time. She's always *there*. And when she makes it plain that she prefers the child of Hilda Runnall to her own granddaughters..."

"Ah, there's the rub. Why can't you let things be? What does it matter if she does prefer Rose Anders? It isn't——" he paused, laughing uncomfortably. "It isn't as if she had any money to leave."

Margaret changed her tactics. "Talking of money, it isn't as if we are letting the State look after her. It will cost us pounds a week, and who knows for how long?"

When a suitable opportunity occurred Margaret tried to put this point of view across to her mother, But Mrs. Beewater refused to be impressed.

CHAPTER 8

Rose was appalled. "Send you to a home? But why? What sort of a home?" The only home she had ever seen was the Battersea Dogs' Home, and that had depressed her considerably; not that the people there weren't kind, indeed they were, but such a terrible number of unwanted dogs all cooped up together seemed to her the last word in dreadfulness, and it wouldn't be any better if all the dogs were unwanted old grannies! "They can't do that to you!" she said. Then her own loss came home to her. "What will I do if you go? Shall I be able to see you?"

She and Mrs. Beewater were sitting in the little shop where they had had their first ice-cream together, talking in low voices like a couple of conspirators. The kind woman behind the counter, though she appeared to be taking no notice, was in fact very well aware that a drama of sorts was being played out under her nose. Mrs. Beewater was quite her favourite customer, and she knew Rose Anders by sight, and the story of her life. Now she saw with pity Mrs. Beewater's sad, set face and Rose's look of anxiety and horror.

"When are you going?" asked Rose.

"On Tuesday."

"And today is Saturday. Oh, Mrs. Beewater—Helena" —another great chasm seemed to yawn across Rose's life —"why don't we do something? Look, why don't you write to your nieces, Lilian's daughters, and ask if you can go and live with them?"

Mrs. Beewater shook her head.

"Your son, Gerard, then."

"He agrees with Margaret that I must go."

Gerard had come over to see her at Margaret's request. He was affable as he always was and appeared to be kind, but his mother knew well enough that his kindness never went deep enough to interfere with his own pleasure or pocket.

"You know we all want to do the best for you, Mother," he had said. "But it's a little difficult to know what to do. Everywhere is so expensive, you see; anywhere that you would fancy, that is. We would like to ask you to come and stay with us," he went on, "but, as you know, we shall be spending several months in South Africa."

"Thank you, my dear," Mrs. Beewater had said, a little smile playing round her lips. Gerard could always say the pleasant thing. He had never asked her to stay since she had given up her flat, afraid, she supposed, that she might become a permanency. In any case she had no wish to live with him and his wife. On the occasions when Helena had stayed there she had spent most of her time in her bedroom, and Gerard had said things which she resented: "If only father had invested wisely. If he had taken my advice he could have avoided death duties. If you hadn't spent all your capital on that expensive flat. If only you would have cut down your expenses..." No. There was no point in looking to Gerard for sympathy or help.

"Let's go and sit in the library," Mrs. Beewater said to Rose as they plodded up the little hill towards the common. She felt suddenly tired. They sat down in the comfortable arm-chairs beside a little round table. There were few people about on this Saturday morning and they could talk undisturbed.

"We can write to each other," Helena suggested.

"Oh, letters!" said Rose contemptuously. She knew all about letters. Daddy wrote to her and Ricky once a month from America, and his letters said exactly nothing. You couldn't *talk* about things in letters.

Mrs. Beewater tried her hardest to look on the bright side, for Rose's sake if not for her own. "Things may not be so bad as I fear," she said. "Perhaps I shall like it— eventually."

"But I shan't ever like you being away," said Rose, quietly but fiercely. This place, The Homestead, was miles away and they would probably never meet again.

"Rose," said Helena, leaning forward.

"Yes?" queried Rose, staring earnestly into her friend's face, and also leaning forward until their heads were nearly touching.

"Before I go I have something I want to give you. The big Bible with the pictures."

"For me? To keep always for my very own?"

"Always, Rose. I want you to have it to remember me by."

"I won't need it for that!" retorted Rose indignantly.

"I want you to have it for another reason too. I've been thinking, Rose, thinking and thinking the last few days— and nights too—and I have come to a conclusion. I've had that Bible all these years and I've never read it. I wish I had. I think if I had things might have been different."

"Different? How?"

"Perhaps," said Helena, very slowly, "*things* wouldn't have been different but maybe *I* would. I have never had time for God, you see, and now it is too late; I'm too old. But you, Rose, you are young and you have all life in front of you and I want everything for you. I want you to be happy and——"

"But you were happy," interrupted Rose. "You've had a lovely life, you've always said so."

"Yes. It's true. I have always been happy—until my husband died."

"Well then. I don't know what you mean."

For some moments Mrs. Beewater sat in silence, staring at the highly polished floor. "It's true I was happy, but then everything went my way. I only thought about myself. Oh, yes, I know I made my husband happy, but when you love someone very much that is no hardship! What I mean is—what I said just now—I never had time for God. He just didn't count and I managed perfectly well without Him just because I had everything. Now I have nothing. Life is over. I've *done* nothing."

"You mean, you can't just go to God now and say— well, say something to put things right."

"Would you like it if someone did that to you?"

"No, I wouldn't, of course; but then," said Rose wisely, "perhaps God is different."

"Perhaps He is," murmured Mrs. Beewater sadly. Then briskly, "Let's go to my room now and I'll give you the Bible."

Three days later, silent and tight-lipped, Mrs. Beewater had packed her cases and made herself ready to go away to The Homestead. She would not allow her daughter to touch anything or help her in any way, and permitted herself to ask one question only:

"What about my books and pictures? And my desk?"

"We thought—well," said Margaret awkwardly. "Mrs. Jenkins is quite willing for you to take some things for your room, a few books and so on, and I told her you particularly loved your little desk; but we'll leave them at the moment until we see how you settle in, shall we? Don't you agree? I mean, it *would* be silly, *wouldn't* it, until we *know* ..."

Mrs. Beewater bent over her packing without comment. Settle in! If she settled at all it would be in despair.

The car was at the door. "Goodbye, Grannie," said the little girls, lifting up their small, pale faces to kiss her.

Robert Steele had said his goodbyes with great heartiness the evening before. "All the very best," he had said;

"we'll see you often, I hope. Let us know if you want anything, and don't worry about a single thing. Everything is going to be all right."

"Come along," cried Margaret gaily. The car door was open and waiting for her, the engine was running.

Mrs. Beewater did not look back as they drove away. After all, she had never regarded the house as her home, but when they passed the Anders' house she turned in her seat and stared at it. There was no sign of life: Hilda Runnall and her husband were no doubt at work, Mum was probably cleaning somewhere out of sight, but Rose and Ricky—where were they?

Margaret Steele drove competently through the towns and traffic, and during the fifteen-mile drive the two women sat for the most part in silence, Mrs. Beewater gazing out of the window. As the car came frequently to a standstill in the traffic jams she watched the women out shopping, coping with the hum-drum of every day; babies in prams, children running along beside them; old people with heavy loads of shopping in string bags; a blind man with a dog; a happy, healthy young woman with a child clinging to each arm and talking nineteen to the dozen. I suppose, thought Mrs. Beewater, looking about at the shabby surburban shopping centre, that I had more to spend in one week than most of these people have in one year. I was lucky enough to find the perfect husband and I lived for him. 'You never had any time for me—I didn't count.' Her daughter's bitter words came back unbidden. Oh, God, was it true? Had she failed her children? Had she, in fact, ever lived for anyone but herself and her own pleasure? She could find no answer to her questions.

"Nearly there," said Mrs. Steele. Her mother roused herself. They had left the shabby streets and were driving along a tree-lined road with pleasant houses surrounded by gardens, and in a couple of minutes Margaret turned the car into a circular drive and drew up at a flight of

steps leading to a large black front door. The house had
once been very handsome indeed. It was spacious with
large, wide windows and two storeys above the ground
floor, but you could see at a glance that it was a long time
since anyone with money had lived there. The paint,
though not blistered, looked tired, and the curtains were
inexpensive and carelessly hung. The garden was neat
but it was obviously years since a gardener had lovingly
made it his life's work to tend it.

Oh, dear, thought Margaret, as she rang the bell. It
does look tatty today in all this sunshine. She glanced
furtively at her mother, whose face was dignified and im-
passive, giving nothing away.

A woman came to the door, smiling widely; Mrs. Jenkins herself. "So this is our new lady: Mrs. Beewater, isn't
it?" she said, holding out her hand. "Come in, dearie."
And scarcely was Mrs. Beewater inside than Mrs. Jenkins
plopped a fat kiss on her cheek. "We have all been looking forward to meeting you—all the old ladies, and our
old gentleman too. He's a darling; you'll love him." She
laughed richly. "Where's your luggage, dear? You haven't
brought *too* much, I hope. It's not a very large room."

While she and Margaret went to the boot to extract the
suitcases, Mrs. Beewater had time to study her new ward-
ress, as she was already calling her in her own mind. She
was plump and dressed in a not unbecoming green nylon
overall. Her feet were enormously broad and there was a
ladder in one stocking. Her hair, which was neat enough,
had been burnished to a brilliant shade of brass, otherwise, Mrs. Beewater surmised, it would have been a
gloomy grey. While observing these details with a complete lack of charity she heard Mrs. Jenkins say, "It'll be a
bit strange to her at first, poor old soul, but give her a
week and she'll settle down and be as happy as Larry,
you'll see." (*Settle down, happy as Larry,* both phrases
Margaret had used!)

"Yes, well——" responded Mrs. Steele, plainly nervous,

not of Mrs. Jenkins of course, but of her mother who was standing perfectly still, like Lot's wife, at the top of the steps.

"Now let's come upstairs, shall we, and see your nice little room," invited Mrs. Jenkins, still smiling, and carrying the heaviest suitcase. "Don't you carry anything, dearie; you just concentrate on getting yourself up the stairs and mind you hold on the banisters. I always tell my old ladies that—we don't want any accidents, I tell them."

Mrs. Beewater and Mrs. Steele followed the broad green back up the stairs and along a passage, which smelt strongly of onions, until she came to a door which she flung open, saying cheerily, "Here we are then. Your dear little room. All to yourself."

A little room it certainly was, a tube almost, with a large window taking up the whole of the end wall. It had obviously been part of a much larger room and the cornices in the ceiling ran into nothing where the division had been made. The window looked out on the gabled roof of what was probably a garage.

There was a large bed up against the left wall, a large old-fashioned wardrobe against the right wall and blocking part of the window, a minute hand-basin, a shabby chest of drawers, and one armchair. There was a carpet of indeterminate colour, rather threadbare, and the curtains and bedspread were of multi-coloured folk-weave. At some time or other damp had caused an unsightly stain on ceiling and wall. The room, however, was clean and smelt fresh.

"There!" said Mrs. Jenkins, plonking down the case. "Welcome to Homesteads, my dear!"

"But," said Mrs. Steele, her mouth opening and shutting helplessly. "But, Mrs. Jenkins, *this* isn't the room you showed me!"

"Oh, you mean the other room, the one facing the other way?"

"I mean a much bigger room, nicer altogether, looking out over the garden and the trees. A *much* nicer room." '

"Ah, that room. Well, yes," said Mrs. Jenkins, her smile becoming rather fixed. "I did show you that room, I know, but you see it did seem rather a waste to have just one lady there when there are so many wanting to come. And then, you see, I didn't hear from you and then another lady wanted to come and I hadn't the heart to turn her away. Poor old soul," she added, while Mrs. Steele was gathering herself together for assault. "So I've got two in that room now."

"What do you *mean*, you didn't hear from me. I telephoned you the same evening about two hours after I had seen you, and I *definitely* booked the room you showed me."

"I had nothing in writing, and you didn't pay a deposit."

"You didn't *ask* me to pay anything in advance, and as for writing I didn't know it was *necessary*. I thought it was a—a—gentlemen's agreement!" Just in time she prevented herself from saying a ladies' agreement, the word lady having figured largely in the conversation.

Mrs. Jenkins decided to be conciliatory. "Well, the fact is, I get so let down. Ladies say they'll have a room and then I don't hear any more and I turn someone away and then I'm left. And it is my living, you know. Perhaps I could take a pound a week off."

"A pound a week!" exploded Margaret. "It's sheer robbery to charge what you're charging for a room like this. There isn't even a bedside lamp!"

"There's a good enough light up there and there's a switch by the bed. See?" Mrs. Jenkins turned it on, and off again immediately, and they all looked up at the ceiling where an electric bulb hung, quite unclothed but with a sort of white plate hanging over its head. "None of my ladies have ever complained. They all like this room.

It's ever so warm, and the bed's comfy. Feel it." She turned back the bedclothes and thumped it vigorously. "And what's more," she went on, straightening her back, "let me tell you, it's not just the room, not the meals even; it's the care I give them. None of my ladies are ever neglected—I help them to bath and do their hair and cut their toe-nails..."

As if she could bear no more, Mrs. Beewater turned and walked to the door, and, uncertainly, fighting a grim battle within herself, Margaret Steele followed her.

"And she won't spend much time in her room, of course," Mrs. Jenkins was saying, hurrying after them. "There's the sitting-room downstairs where all the ladies sit, and our gentleman too. Just come and see the rest of the house. You'd like to see it, wouldn't you, dearie?" At the head of the party once more she led the way, showing them the bathroom, 'another lady's room' which she entered without knocking, and then downstairs to the sitting-room.

It could have been a pleasant room: it was large, with a lofty ceiling and french windows leading out to a lawn with flower-beds all round it, but near the window was a square table with a seersucker cloth on it, laid ready for the mid-day dinner. The other end of the room was furnished with arm-chairs and a sofa round a hideous fireplace with an enormous yellowing mirror above it. There was a tired-looking fern in a pot, a vase full of pampas grass which looked as if it had not been touched for years, and another vase of assorted artificial flowers of brilliant hues.

"Here are my ladies and my gentleman," announced Mrs. Jenkins, smiling widely once more. "We're just one happy family and ever so snug, aren't we, dears?"

The old people nodded their heads, smiling gently. They were not very old; that is, none was crippled or infirm or senile or dirty or badly dressed. Neither did they look unhappy or unpleasant. But to Helena Beewater so much old age in one room presented a picture of utter despair. She would be stifled, she thought, if she sat here all day; she would go mad with depression if she sat upstairs in 'her' room staring at the slates of the garage roof.

Margaret Steele pulled herself together and produced her own sweet smile.

"Good morning," she said kindly to the old people.

"Good morning," they chorused, smiling, in their turn.

"Isn't it a lovely bright day?"

"Lovely today, isn't it?"

"Better than yesterday. What a downpour!"

"But the wind is still cold."

"Well, so long as it doesn't rain..."

"Yes, it's nice if you can go out a little..."

"I usually sit in the garden every day..."

Oh no! thought Mrs. Beewater. Not this—Oh God, not this! Standing perfectly still, her face expressionless, she began to pray within herself with all the force of which she was capable. God help me! Take me out of this! Make Margaret do something...

A moment or two later she found they were standing in the hall, the door of the sitting-room closed (for ever, she hoped) behind them. What now? Almighty God, please do something! A miracle, please, please...

Seeing her daughter and Mrs. Jenkins facing each other and about to argue, Mrs. Beewater turned away.

"I am not satisfied, Mrs. Jenkins."

"I'm sure I don't know why you're not."

"You know exactly. You promised me a much nicer room."

"I didn't promise you anything except that I'd look after your mother because you couldn't be bothered to do it yourself." Here Margaret began to protest but Mrs. Jenkins shouted her down. "She's got a single room, something everyone wants and can't have, and a very nice little room too, though I say it. She'll have every care here and you'll be relieved of the worry. I mean, that's worth paying for, isn't it, and I told you I'd charge you less for the room."

"If you reduced it by ten pounds I wouldn't allow my mother to stay," said Margaret in a cold fury. "Kindly bring her cases down at once. Make haste, please. I'm in a hurry to get away. Come, Mother."

The miracle! It had happened! And without any help from Mrs. Beewater. Throughout the whole interview she had not said one word.

CHAPTER 9

Richard was home from hospital by this time and it was a problem to know how to keep him occupied. He had been sent away for a fortnight's convalescence, which he had not particularly enjoyed, but his arm was still in plaster and he was having rather troublesome headaches. His mother provided him with everything she thought he could possibly want and had even stayed at home with him one whole day. Jack too was kind, taking him out in the evenings sometimes, and at weekends they all went out together. And Mum, the valuable Mrs. Mumford, did her best to spoil him unmercifully. It was Rose, however, who really looked after him and put up with his irritable moods, and obeyed his lordly commands, and fetched and carried, and played draughts and a multitude of other games with him.

They were up in their day room. The radio was on but neither Ricky nor Rose was listening to it. The table was littered with a half-finished jig-saw puzzle, books, magazines and a chemistry set, and while Ricky was listlessly doodling Rose stood by the window staring out over the common at the care-free dogs and strutting pigeons. The emptiness of the long holidays from school had arrived. Suddenly she gave a little cry.

"What?" said Richard, startled.

"Mrs. Beewater!"

"I thought she was locked up in a home."

"She is. She was! But that's her all right." Rose rushed from the room and down the stairs and a few seconds later was standing looking up at her friend's face.

"Did you think I was a ghost?"

"I wanted you so badly and then—there you were!"

"I didn't go to the home after all. Or rather, I did but I didn't stay."

"Oh, marvellous!" cried Rose, jumping up and down. "So now you're going to stay here for ever."

"I shouldn't think so. No, I'm sure I shan't do that."

Rose's face fell. "Why not? Won't Mrs. Steele let you?"

"Let's get out of this wind. I never met such a draughty place as this common."

"You can come to our house," said Rose eagerly. "No one's there except Ricky—oh, and Mum, of course, but she's cooking. Anyway, she wouldn't mind. Come on."

Slowly they made their way back to the tall house, talking all the time. Mum looked out of the kitchen and nodded to Mrs. Beewater, who smiled graciously.

Richard stood up as they entered the day room. "Well, Ricky, this *is* nice," said Mrs. Beewater. "It's such a long time since we have met. How is the arm?" They talked for a little about Ricky's aches and pains and his experiences in hospital, and then Rose, at Ricky's command, went to make some coffee. "I really oughtn't to have to tell you about a thing like that," he said severely.

"Well, what *is* going to happen to you?" asked Rose anxiously, having produced the Nescafé and biscuits.

Mrs. Beewater shook her head.

"You've got to live somewhere," said Ricky.

"Alas, yes," agreed Mrs. Beewater. "But I think—I have the feeling—that everything is going to be all right."

"How?" demanded Rose.

Mrs. Beewater looked out into the distance across the common to the big main road, and further still to the trees the other side, her thoughts obviously far away. She said slowly, "It was odd, you know. I prayed. In that home my daughter took me to. It was so awful. I thought if I had to stay there I should die. My spirit anyway would die. There was nothing I could do. I don't think I said anything all the time. I just prayed. I asked Almighty God to do something."

"And what did He do?" the children chorused, open-mouthed.

"Margaret changed her mind."

"I don't think you can say God did anything," said Ricky judiciously. "I mean, Margaret changed her mind. So what? It would have been the same anyway."

"No," returned Mrs. Beewater firmly. "I can't explain it; I just have a conviction. I'm not given to praying, as you may have guessed. I have never been a religious woman, but I suddenly felt I must pray—as if the divine presence were there, waiting——" She stopped abruptly, and then, as if having started she had to finish, "and as if it is still there, all about me."

"What is?" asked Ricky.

"I don't know." And indeed, she didn't, because as far as her circumstances were concerned nothing was one whit better.

She had been back in the Steeles' house for two days, and though everyone, including Margaret, was polite and kind there was an 'atmosphere', a sense that she was being talked about behind closed doors. She did not know whether to unpack her cases and to treat the incident as if it had never happened; or whether to discuss things frankly with her daughter. And so the days passed with polite exchanges on both sides, but there was no warmth of spirit, no laughter, no spontaneity. Margaret really did want to do the right thing, but she was in a real dilemma: the family were going to Scotland shortly, and their arrangements did not include Mrs. Beewater.

Then, at last, at almost the eleventh hour, a 'vacancy occurred' at a home only a few miles away. It was not exactly a home but more of a private hotel for elderly people of both sexes. Margaret Steele had liked it very much previously but had regretfully refused to consider it because it was too expensive. She had, however, thought it wise to keep her mother's name on the waiting list.

"So you see, Mother," she said, "there's nothing for it but for you to take the vacancy—just temporarily. Unfortunately we can't afford to keep you there for long. I say 'unfortunately'," she corrected herself hastily, "because it really is a nice place."

"I seem to have heard the word 'nice' before in this connection," observed Mrs. Beewater drily.

Margaret tossed her head. "All right then. Never let me forget The Homestead, will you? This place is good, pleasant, in good taste and hideously expensive." And she went out of the room, not slamming the door but shutting it extremely firmly behind her. Really! Mothers were impossible! Robert was being tiresome too, grumbling about the price, insisting that it would be cheaper and less trouble all round to take her with them to Scotland or to put her in a moderately-priced hotel. They had nearly quarrelled.

"Understand this, Robert," Margaret had said, "Mother has *got* to get *used* to the idea of a home. She is just on eighty, she needs care and attention, she will need more and I want to get her settled before that time comes. If I put her in a hotel she will want to stay there and we can't afford it, and I will *not* have her at home indefinitely."

"What care and attention does she need? I've never met a younger old lady. You don't do more for her than you do for me; less, in fact."

"How can you *possibly* know? *Every* old lady needs care and attention—or if she doesn't now she soon will and I can't and won't undertake it. I have you and the girls to look after and—and all my outside work—and—and everything."

So, fearing tears, Robert retired. "She's your mother, not mine." And on that unsatisfactory note the argument ended never to be reopened.

"I think," said Mrs. Beewater to Rose later that day, "that I shall have to come back because they can't afford to keep me there for long. But what will happen after that I don't know. Margaret is determined to get rid of me."

"I wish you were my granny," said Rose. "I'd see you weren't sent away."

That night Rose found it hard to sleep. She worried about her friend; she worried on her own account too, knowing how terribly she would miss her—this old lady (who didn't seem old) who now meant far more to her than her own mother. She worried too, without being able to put it into words, about the uncertainty of life. You could never be quite sure about anything.

Thinking about Mrs. Beewater she remembered the big black Bible with the Harold Copping pictures in it. She had been reading it quite a lot recently, looking at the pictures and turning up the references underneath them, not always understanding what she read but loving the sound and beauty of the words. And Mrs. Beewater, dear Helena, had asked her to read it. Very well then, she would. She turned on her bedside lamp and began to read it again.

As so often happened, she found herself looking at the picture of *The Little Child Set in the Midst*. The big Bible seemed to open there by itself. There was the man with the kind face, the little child, boy or girl, sitting on his knee looking utterly contented and comfortable and safe. Nothing could happen to him while he was sitting there with the man's arms around him. Tonight, Rose thought, the little boy sitting by himself on the steps above looked very much alone and as if he too would like to be surrounded by those strong arms. I'm outside too, Rose told herself, and I don't want to be! Jesus called a little child unto Him, and set him in the midst of them. Jesus, Jesus, her heart cried out, I want to come to you too. I want to be in your arms, safe and happy. Let me come too, Jesus; and it seemed to her that there was an answer, as if the Friend of children had said, "Come, Rose, I want you too. I love you and I'll look after you!" And presently she fell asleep, very, very content.

CHAPTER 10

Haven Hill was certainly different from The Homestead. It could scarcely have been more different. Each of the guests (they were called 'guests', not 'old ladies' or 'old gentlemen') had single rooms, tastefully furnished, with central heating, an electric fire, and an electric kettle beside a tray of tea-things always ready for use. The beds were comfortable and there was a washbasin in each room. No. 7, Mrs. Beewater's room, faced north and overlooked the front garden and the road to the houses on the other side. It was quite a mile from the town and the road was always very quiet, very still, with only an occasional car passing up or down it. It seemed to Helena that nothing ever happened there.

Haven Hill itself was very quiet too. The place was run efficiently with no fuss and no bother, by an army of white-coated dailies who did what was expected of them, no more and no less. Lunch was served downstairs every day at separate tables carefully laid, and the meals were adequate but uninteresting. Apart from lunch, to which everyone was expected to come unless ill in bed, all the other meals were served upstairs on trays in the bedrooms. The staff were instructed not to get 'involved' with the guests.

"Well, I suppose this is very 'nice'," Helena told herself as she sat up in bed having breakfast, on the first day.

"I suppose I can bear this," she told herself at lunchtime while listening and taking a polite part in the aimless and spiritless conversation which flowed from table to table.

"I suppose I must be thankful for small mercies," she told herself, sighing with boredom, as she sat by the electric fire in her bedroom, eating the tinned peaches and cream on her supper tray.

But by her third day at Haven Hill she had decided that she couldn't bear it and that she refused to be thankful for the small mercies of a comfortable prison. True, it was not a prison, and she had perfect freedom to do as she liked and go out when she liked, but she did not feel inclined to amuse herself all day, neither did she feel able to be always out of doors.

So what did her day at Haven Hill consist of? Breakfast in bed, bath, dress slowly, read the newspaper and listen to something on the radio, go down to lunch and make polite conversation, have an afternoon nap, make a cup of tea and listen to the radio again, supper at seven in her room, television downstairs with the other guests: if you could bear it—then bed again. What sort of a life was that? The fact that many women of her age were content with just such a life was no answer at all. Mrs. Beewater was not.

An idea was gradually taking shape in her mind.

At the same time as Mrs. Beewater was feeling lonely and unhappy in her room, Ricky and Rose after four weeks' holiday from school were also feeling dissatisfied with life in general. They also were tired of amusing themselves. They had been out all the morning so they didn't particularly want to go out again. What to, anyway? It was a cold blustery day with a grey sky, not in the least like summer, and it would certainly rain if the wind dropped. Seeing a pack of cards lying on the table Ricky picked them up and hurled them at the wall across the room, where they lay scattered about on the carpet. He and Rose began to quarrel as to who should pick them up.

"Oh-h-h," said Ricky with a long yawn that turned into a groan. It was Monday afternoon. On the previous Saturday Mummy and Jack had taken both children to a matinee, after which they had gone out somewhere to dinner. Then on the Sunday Jack had taken them miles and miles in the car and they had had tea at a quaint little café in the country. No, the weekends weren't too bad, because Mummy and Jack were around, but the five days between one weekend and the next seemed never-ending. Now even Mum had gone home.

"Hey, tell you what!" said Rose suddenly.

Richard looked at her brightening face with a degree of interest, and Rose went on, "Let's go and see Helena."

"Mrs. Beewater?"

"Yes! Come on, Ricky. Let's!"

"How can we?"

"It's not very far. Well, not *very* far. I know where it is, more or less, and Helena told me—we can get a bus. Come on!"

Richard looked critically at his sister. It always annoyed him when she had the bright ideas, and he told himself that it wasn't a particularly good one. He liked Mrs. Beewater all right, very much actually, but ... well —what else was there to do?

"All right," he said. "But you'd better change into something decent. You know Mrs. Beewater doesn't like jeans, and that sweater has a hole in it—did you know?"

"And you'd better wash your face," retorted Rose. "You've got Biro all over it—did *you* know?"

For once Rose took trouble to make herself look nice. She chose a warm-ish red dress which she knew her darling Helena had admired, she washed her face and hands and brushed her straight yellow hair until it shone. Then she put on a decent pair of shoes and gazed at herself in the long mirror in her mother's room. "It's true," she told herself; "I do look better when I'm properly dressed, but it's too much bother to do it always."

"Have you got some money, Ricky?"

"Yes, I've got some money."

They slammed the front door behind them and, harmony restored, walked quickly down the road to the bus stop, happy to have an object in view. They hadn't long to wait for the bus, and they hopped on, chattering, and made their way to the front seat at the top.

"All the way," Richard told the conductor. "And when we get there," he said to Rose, "how do we get to Haven Hill?"

"We'll find it," returned Rose confidently, referring to a piece of paper in her pocket with the address written on it in Mrs. Beewater's writing. And so they did, eventually, but it was a long tramp up and down long streets and, in spite of the cool wind, they were hot and tired by the time they found themselves ringing the bell at the highly-polished front door of Haven Hill. The white-coated assistant who opened it looked surprised and doubtful when they asked to see Mrs. Beewater.

"She expecting you?"

"No, but she'll see us. Tell her it's Rose."

"And Richard," added Ricky.

The children were left on the door-step while the white coat swished away to enquire, and some minutes passed before she came back and said she would take them to Mrs. Beewater's room. "She your granny?"

"No," said Rose, and they followed her upstairs.

Mrs. Beewater met them on the landing outside her door, her arms wide open. She and Rose hugged each other, then Mrs. Beewater held out her hand to Ricky and before she knew what she was doing had hugged him too. It seemed like a year since they had met.

The children walked round her room looking critically and interestedly at everything in it. Rose examined the silver brushes, mirror and scentbottles on the dressing-table, saying delightedly, "These are exactly the same as before, aren't they, but they look different here; and where are all your books?" Ricky meanwhile was turning on and off the strip lighting over the gleaming mirror and wash-basin.

"Well, now, come and sit down," said Mrs. Beewater, having arranged the chairs near the window, "and tell me all the news. I've been such a long time shut up in this prison."

"It's not a bad prison," said Richard, looking about him.

"Anywhere is a prison if you are shut up in it," said Mrs. Beewater, "but don't let us talk about it. Tell me about you. How did you come here?"

"Bus."

"Very clever of you to have found your way. I'm *so* glad you did! What have you been doing since I saw you last?"

"Nothing," said Ricky and Rose flatly, forgetting all about their weekend activities or deciding that they were not worth mentioning.

"And that is what I have been doing," said Mrs. Beewater. "Exactly nothing. There's nothing to do. I get up and I go to bed and I read my newspaper and I have a rest—rest from what? And one day, I suppose, I shall walk down the High Street and buy some stamps and come home again and have another rest!"

For the next half hour they talked companionably about nothing very much, and then Mrs. Beewater made some tea.

"There are exactly three drops of milk," she said, peering into the tiny jug, "so we can have one each; and I have some biscuits—in that tin behind you, Richard—and we'll pretend that I am taking you out to tea at Harrods..." She began to talk about the past. Rose, of course, listened with the greatest interest, but Richard soon got busy with his own thoughts.

Presently he heard Mrs. Beewater say, "But I shall only be here for a short time, I suppose," and he roused himself to ask, "Then what?"

Mrs. Beewater fiddled with a strand of her beautiful white hair and was silent. The children waited. She was so obviously lost in thought.

"Come on," said Rose at length. "Do tell us!"

The old lady looked at the two young faces; her clear eyes scrutinised first one then the other as if she were trying to make up her mind.

"I have an idea," she said.

"Yes, well tell us!" urged Rose, bouncing up and down in her chair.

"Shush!" said Richard impatiently.

"I have a friend," began Mrs. Beewater slowly. "My husband and I have known him for years. We didn't meet often, you understand, but we always kept in touch, and occasionally after a long time abroad we would go and spend a few days with him in his rectory, and once he spent a month with us in Nairobi. I wrote to tell him of my husband's death and he wrote me a very sweet little letter saying that if he could help me in any way he always would."

"So?" queried Richard.

There was a long silence which even the impatient Rose did not dare to break.

"I keep thinking about him. I wonder ... I believe he would advise me. He is too good a friend to let me remain in this hopeless position—in a home or in my daughter's house—unwanted."

"But how could he help you?" asked Rose.

"I don't know," said Mrs. Beewater slowly, as if she were a long way away. "But he said he would help me, and he loved my husband very dearly. He is the Rector of Little St. Paul's in Sussex, and he has a lovely old rectory with a walled garden and rooks' nests in the trees. I can hear those rooks now—and smell the new-mown grass, and the roses—you know, those lovely English smells. The warm sun on the pine needles ... When you've been out of England for a long time you notice those things."

She was in another world now, a long way from the prim room.

"I think I'll go and see him," she said, leaning back in her chair.

"Couldn't you write?" suggested Richard. "I mean, it's a long way to go, and he might be away or something."

"It wouldn't be much use writing. The dear man isn't very practical. Not business-like. He used to write to my husband occasionally but he never *answered* letters. If I could talk to him though, he would understand and would advise me."

"How far is Sussex?" asked Rose.

"Well, Brighton isn't far," said Richard, who had been there once.

"But Little St. Paul's isn't near Brighton," said Mrs. Beewater. "It's nearer Hampshire, and if you go by train you have to change and then get a bus because there is no station there. We used to get a taxi in the old days, or he would come and meet us."

Rose had been thinking hard. "But have you enough money to go such a long way?" She glanced uncertainly at Helena as Richard kicked her ankle hard, scowling ferociously.

Helena smiled reassuringly. "I sold a ring recently, so for the moment I am fairly comfortable. But don't tell anyone I said so!"

"But—but"—Rose was still anxious for her friend—"will Mrs. Steele let you go?"

"Oh, Rose, shut up!" said Richard. "You do say the most frightful things!"

Rose's face flushed a delicate pink and Mrs. Beewater patted her hand. "I've thought of that too. Margaret won't know. I shall go tomorrow."

"Tomorrow!" gasped both the children together.

"Yes, tomorrow. Talking it over with you has decided me. I'll go tomorrow." She rose from her chair a new wo-man, a woman with a purpose, and opening her wardrobe she took out a small over-night case and began to put things in it.

"I really think," said Richard carefully, "that you wouldn't be wise to go *tomorrow*. When you're going on a journey," he explained, "you have to make arrangements."

Mrs. Beewater, having spent most of life travelling in many parts of the world, found this too delightful, and she laughed, a youthful sparkle in her eyes.

"I mean," said Richard gravely and loudly, "what about trains? And where will you go from? You must think a little bit, Mrs. Beewater!"

"You know, you're rather a sensible person," said Mrs. Beewater, sitting down again and becoming quite serious. "It's true, I shall have to think a little bit. Tomorrow I'll get a time-table. Today's Monday. Yes, I'll lay my plans tomorrow, Ricky, as you so excellently advise, and go on Wednesday. I'll tell them I'll be out to lunch, and that I'm going to see a friend. I suppose they will have to be told that much."

Rose eyed the little pig-skin case. "Are you going to stay the night?"

"Well, I don't know. I might. But I should have thought I ought to be able to manage it in one day."

"Madame would certainly worry if you were away all night," remarked Rose.

"If I couldn't get back I should telephone. Yes, I must remember to take the number with me."

"Why don't you phone *him* from here to tell him you're coming. It would be safer, you know." Advice again from Ricky.

But Mrs. Beewater would have none of it. "No," she said firmly. "I don't know his number, and it would be awkward telephoning from here. The phone is in the hall and quite public." She was a stubborn old lady who was quite accustomed to making up her mind and acting upon it, and the plan had taken such a firm hold of her imagination that nothing would shake her determination.

An idea was now taking hold of Rose, and, when Mrs. Beewater went again to rummage among her possessions in her chest of drawers, Rose leaned over to whisper in Ricky's ear. He pushed her away.

"Listen!" she hissed at him.

"Silly!" he hissed back at her. "Of course we can't!"

"We can! We can, Ricky!"

"They'd never let us."

"Course they wouldn't, so we don't ask, see?"

"What are you two plotting?" Mrs. Beewater enquired, the whispering having become as loud as whispers could.

"Rose says we're coming with you," Ricky volunteered at length.

"Oh, yes, yes! Mrs. Beewater, Helena dear, do let us," pleaded Rose.

"I am quite sure your mother wouldn't approve."

Rose was quite sure too. But she knew how to get round that little problem. She also knew that Helena had no idea that Rose's mother had forbidden her to see anything more of the Steele family, including the Steele grandmother.

"You know they wouldn't let us," said Richard.

Rose took no notice of him. "Do you realise, Helena, that if we don't come with you, you'll be entirely alone? And anything, *anything* could happen to you!"

"D'you know what? I love you both for caring about me!" cried Mrs. Beewater, smiling with joy. "But I can't possibly let you go so far from home without your mother's permission."

"Leave it to me," said Rose. "I'll fix it."

CHAPTER 11

And so the adventure began. They had laid their plans very carefully.

On the Monday Ricky had been down to the local station to make all the necessary enquiries about the times of trains there and back, where to change, the cost of fares, and so on, and it looked as if they could easily be at Little St. Paul's by mid-day. The Rector and Mrs. Beewater would have their little chat while Ricky and Rose explored the village and got something to eat, and then they would be home in time for supper with Mummy and Jack. A lovely day and no questions asked. "And if we are not home," said Rose, "Mummy never minds us being out late so long as she knows where we are."

"If she knows where we are she'll be very cross indeed. What are you going to tell her?"

"I'm going to leave her a note: 'Ricky and I are spending the day with Helena.' She won't know who Helena is. She'll simply think it's one of my girl-friends. Which it is," finished Rose virtuously.

"No word of a lie," said Richard, quoting Mum.

"No word of a lie to anyone," agreed Rose.

And so, on the Wednesday, the conspirators met at Victoria Station at 9.30 to catch the 9.45 train. Everything worked out according to plan. As usual Mummy and Jack left the house by eight o'clock, and Mum would not arrive before half past nine. Rose left her note propped up on the kitchen table so that Mum would see it first and, if the children did happen to be late, Mummy would see it when she got home in the evening.

Mrs. Beewater arrived at the station on time, composed and happy and looking very trim. Rose too had dressed carefully for the occasion and had brought a jolly-looking plastic bag with some chocolate, a few apples, one or two packets of Spangles and a few comics to read on the journey. She had considered bringing a picnic lunch but Mrs. Beewater had assured them that they would have 'eggs in the kitchen' at the rectory.

It was going to be a wonderful day, and no one would be any the wiser. And Mrs. Beewater, dear Helena, would be so happy when she had talked things over with her friend, the Rector of Little St. Paul's, whose name was the Reverend Rupert Allendale. Rose had gathered, though Mrs. Beewater certainly had not said so, that Mr. Allendale had not only been fond of Mr. Beewater but had also been terribly fond of Helena herself and would do anything for her. And he had never married, had he; a housekeeper had looked after him ... So?

Rose sighed contentedly. Helena's life-story would have a perfect ending.

It was well after one o'clock when they arrived at Little St. Paul's because latterly things had not worked out according to plan. When they left the train at the junction there was no connection. Richard argued with the porter about it, and the porter at last grew cross and said, "All right then, sit and wait for it; wait all night if you like, but the only way to get to Little St. Paul's is to take a bus, and you'd better look sharp as the bus'll be going any minute." So they hurried along to the bus station, but the bus didn't even come in for another twenty minutes and there was nowhere to sit down. Mrs. Beewater grew very tired and lamented that she had only two legs to stand on, while Ricky muttered darkly about the ticket man at the station near Haven Hill who had given them wrong information. Rose dived into her bag and brought out apples and Spangles to ease matters, but Mrs. Beewater did not eat apples in the street, and Richard bit into a nest of insects and disgustedly threw his away.

The bus did come eventually, however, and the sun shone cheerfully on the lovely Sussex countryside which, to Rose's eyes, looked enchanting after London.

When the rackety bus drew up at its terminal there was another long wait for the one and only taxi to take them to the Rectory three miles away. Mrs. Beewater was by that time in a great state of tension and kept looking anxiously at her watch. But at last the taxi came and the three bundled into it. The driver knew the Rectory well but seemed surprised they were going there. "It's all shut up," he said. "Least it was. P'raps the new rector's come, has he?"

Richard glanced quickly at Mrs. Beewater but she evidently had not heard this statement and Richard did not feel like repeating it to her. Having come so far, better let things take their course, he thought.

"Dear me," said Mrs. Beewater as they turned in at the drive, "it *has* gone downhill. It used to be so beautifully kept."

"There hasn't been anyone living here, not since the last rector went," volunteered the driver, bringing the car to a smooth stop at the front door, "and that's some little time now. Things do get overgrown mighty soon, don't they?"

"What?" demanded Mrs. Beewater, sitting bolt upright. "*What* did you say?"

"I said things soon get overgrown like," repeated the man abashed. "Shall I wait to take you back?"

"No, no!" said Mrs. Beewater, getting neatly out of the car. "How much do I owe you?"

"He says the Rector has gone away," said Richard in a low voice. "'Hadn't he better wait?"

"In that case I must have information," said Mrs. Beewater, not yet feeling this knock-out blow; and with great dignity she paid the driver and wished him good afternoon. When the taxi was safely outside the gate she

turned and looked up at the old house. It certainly did
not look inhabited though there were curtains at the
windows and one or two were slightly open. Imperiously
she pressed the bell in the wide porch and waited. Dole-
fully it rang through the house and when it had died
away she pressed it firmly again. There was no answer.

Standing there silently in the porch Rose thought, Eggs
in the kitchen! She was now very hungry. Richard
thought, Of all the daft things! Now what do we do?
While poor Helena Beewater thought as she clasped and
unclasped her hands over her handbag, It isn't true! It
can't be true! I just don't believe it.

"Come," she said, "we'll go round to the back of the
house." The children followed her to the back door. And
that was open.

"May we come in?" cried Mrs. Beewater pushing it
slightly. There was no reply. They peered inside. Obviously no one lived there now.

But something attracted Rose's attention. There was a
white flutter through the bushes which lined the pathway
leading from the back door to the kitchen garden.
"Look!" she said, nudging Mrs. Beewater's arm. Mrs.
Beewater withdrew her neat head from the doorway and
her eyes followed Rose's pointing finger. A woman, stout
and untidy, wearing a white apron, was coming up the
path carrying in the crook of her arm a large cabbage. She
eyed the trio curiously as she approached, but said nothing.

"Good afternoon," said Mrs. Beewater, inclining her
head slightly.

" 'Ternoon," returned the woman, a question in her
voice.

"We have come to see the Rector."

The woman shook her head.

"The Reverend Rupert Allendale."

No answer, but another shake of the untidy head.

"Where is he?" demanded Mrs. Beewater sharply.

"In America, I think. I did hear he'd gone there. Living with a niece. You friends of his?"

"Certainly we are friends of his! And I can't think he would have gone to America without—without letting me know."

"Ah, well," said the woman with another shake of the head, shifting the cabbage to her other arm. There was a depth of meaning in those two words and in the way she was looking at the three intruders.

"You will kindly tell me what you know," said Mrs. Beewater, her chin lifted.

"Don't know much," said the woman, shrugging. "He wasn't well. Got past it—you know. People did talk but I never took no notice. I don't actually live in Little St. Paul's, see."

"Then what are you doing here?" asked Mrs. Beewater.

"I take care of the place, if you must know. They pay me to keep me eyes on things."

Her head still high, Mrs. Beewater turned and walked down the drive, the children behind her. Outside the gate she turned right, the opposite way from which the taxi had come, and in a minute or two they came to a charming village green with houses, large and small, scattered around it.

"Just as I remembered it," said Mrs. Beewater, and added faintly, "The seat is still there. Let's go and sit down and think what's best to be done."

It was an old-fashioned, wooden seat given in memory of some village benefactor, and thankfully the three settled themselves on it, Mrs. Beewater appropriating one end where she leaned her head wearily on her arm and gave herself up to thought.

Rose, sitting in the middle, carefully divided one of the slabs of chocolate. Mrs. Beewater waved it away, but Rose and Ricky fell on it ravenously and munched contentedly for a minute or two. Then a movement beside Rose and a kind of choked sob made her turn, and she found Mrs.

Beewater crying helplessly into her handkerchief. The remains of the chocolate slid to the ground as Rose snuggled up to her. "Don't cry, Helena. Don't cry, please! Everything will be all right." At which poor Helena cried more than ever. Then Richard came and stood on her other side, stroking her arm, and saying gently, "Mrs. Beewater", over and over again.

Presently the sobs ceased and the old lady began to mop her eyes.

"It really doesn't help to cry," said Richard gently.

"No, it really doesn't," agreed Mrs. Beewater, sniffing. She had not realised until now how much, how very much, she had been counting on the Reverend Rupert Allendale. Now he too had gone, and who would help her? Whoever could? She remembered mournfully the last time she had visited Little St. Paul's, when her husband had been with her, soon after their return from Nairobi. Then she had had love and security and friendship and money, and never an inkling of the sorry things which would befall her in the future. The tears began to fill her eyes and brim over again.

"You must stop crying. It really doesn't help, you know," said Richard, still kindly but more firmly. His sister was now looking white and distressed and about to burst into tears herself. What an impossible situation!

He was wrong about Rose, however. She wasn't going to cry. Getting up from the seat she stood in front of Mrs. Beewater, pressing herself against her knees. "Mrs. Beewater," she said clearly, "you prayed once, remember? You told us about it. And God answered, you know, and you didn't have to stay in that home. Why don't we try praying now? I mean, we could *try*."

"Don't be silly, Rose," said Richard.

Mrs. Beewater was silent for a little while, then with a final mop at her eyes she opened her bag and put away her handkerchief. "Yes, Rose. Thank you for reminding me. We'll try it."

"You can't pray here!" exclaimed Ricky in dismay. "Rose, you really are an ass!"

"Richard doesn't know about praying," explained Rose quickly; "so he can just keep out of it. Ricky, go and sit on the other end of the seat." But Ricky refused to budge.

"You start," said Mrs. Beewater.

"I—I don't know how to," faltered Rose. "You do it," she pleaded. "And do hurry. I'm so terribly hungry!"

"You must be, my dear! All right, I'll start." And remembering the Minnie Barnes of her childhood, she put her hands together and looked up at the blue sky. "Our Father which art in heaven—give us this day our daily bread. We are all very hungry and disappointed and we don't know what to do. We think you can help us. For thine is the kingdom, the power and the glory for ever and ever, Amen. Now you, Rose."

And Rose, after a silence, twisting her hands, said, "Please help us, God. There isn't anyone else. And if You really are like the man the little child was sitting on the knee of, You will look after us, won't You?"

"And how much good will that do?" asked Richard suspiciously, when Rose had finished.

"You wouldn't understand," said Rose.

Meanwhile at home everything was going on very much as usual. Mrs. Mumford had found Rose's note and had left it where it was. Helena, she thought; that's that old lady, bless me if it isn't, what used to be in and out of here at one time. Well, if they're with her they ought to be all right. "Still, I don't like it," she said severely to her vegetables, "kids ought to be looked after, tha's wha' *I* think. They shouldn't be so much on their own; there'll be trouble one of these fine days!"

At Haven Hill one of the white coats was reporting to Madame in the kitchen. "No coffee for No. 7. Out to lunch too."

Madame looked up from the trifle she was making. "She never said anything to me about being out to lunch. Where has she gone?"

"Never said. Come to think of it, she was up and dressed when I took her breakfast tray in. Usually she has it in bed. And she left most of it."

"They should tell me," complained Madame, compressing her lips. "After all, I am responsible for them."

When evening came, the usual supper tray was taken up to room No. 7, and was collected untouched at 7.30. The senior white coat, who slept in the house, then telephoned Madame, who slept in her own home two miles away.

"Telephone me again at nine," said Madame. At 9.30 she was round at Haven Hill peering into Mrs. Beewater's wardrobe. "Her clothes are still here, so it doesn't look as if she intended to go for good, which is even more worrying, because something must have happened. Now what do I do? The daughter is up in Scotland." She went downstairs grumbling: "I can't keep her after this." (It never occurred to her that the occupant of No. 7 did not wish to be kept.)

"There were two children here on Monday."

"Who were they? Grandchildren?"

"They said they weren't."

Madame sniffed. "Did they give their names? No? A lot of use that is then!"

Madame was really in a difficulty. She couldn't allow an elderly lady in her care to stay out all night without trying to find out where she was; she did not wish to telephone Mrs. Steele, thus spoiling her holiday in Scotland; she hesitated still more to inform the police. So what to do?

Jack Runnall got home about six o'clock and went straight upstairs to have a bath. He noticed that Ricky and Rose were not about but thought nothing of it—they so often weren't. Mum of course, had gone. Hilda Runnall returned home, a little late, soon after seven and went almost immediately to dish up the dinner which Mum had left in a cool oven.

"Seen the children?" she called to Jack, and then saw Rose's note propped up on the kitchen table. Who is Helena? she thought. And then, glancing at her watch, Whoever she is, they ought to be home by now. She and Jack had their dinner alone, and Hilda cleared away and stacked the dishes for Mum to wash up in the morning. Then they settled down comfortably, Hilda with her glossy magazines, Jack in front of the television. At eight-thirty Hilda sat up, the magazines sliding to the floor.

"Jack, those children ought to be home by now!"

"Sure they ought," returned Jack, his eyes still glued to his television.

Hilda Runnall began to walk round the house, fiddled once or twice with her hair by any mirror she happened to be passing, turned out the gas in the cooker, and finally put through two telephone calls to mothers of children who might possibly be leading her own astray. Then, having discovered nothing, she got out the car and drove round to Mrs. Mumford's house.

"I don't know any more'n what you do," said Mum. "I saw the note. They'd gone, you see, by the time I'd got there this morning."

"So they have been out all day!" exclaimed Hilda in dismay. "Who is Helena, d'you know? I don't remember a child with that name."

Mum wrinkled her forehead and rubbed her nose. From the little that Rose had said she guessed that Mrs. Runnall wouldn't be best pleased to know who Helena was. Still, you had to speak, hadn't you, when there might have been an accident or something. "I think it's that old lady Rose is so fond of."

"Mrs. . . . ?"

"Beewater," supplied Mum, noting the dark colour

flood into her employer's face, and thinking, My, she's a one when her monkey's up and no mistake!

Hilda Runnall marched straight out of the house without another word. At home she seized the telephone and dialled the Steele's number. The bell rang and rang.

CHAPTER 12

Unknown to the three on the green at Little St. Paul's, they had been closely observed. Very little, in fact, could go on in the village without someone's seeing it and putting it away for future reference or immediately passing it on to a neighbour. And in a place where everyone knew everyone else, three strangers, one of them crying bitterly, could scarcely go unnoticed. A Mrs. Pummett living in a small cottage only a hundred yards from the seat on the green had caught sight of the three as they sat down on it and had watched them closely from behind her curtains for several minutes. She was not merely curious—she was also kindly, and there seemed to be trouble. Eventually she emerged from her front door and crossed the grass towards them. The children looked at her blankly. Mrs. Beewater tried to compose her face.

"Er . . ." said Mrs. Pummett.

"Good afternoon," said Mrs. Beewater, with an attempt at a smile.

"I—er—excuse me, but I wondered if something was the matter."

Mrs. Beewater, Ricky and Rose looked at each other.

"I—er—don't want to interfere—you know—but—can I do anything?"

"Perhaps you can tell us," said Mrs. Beewater, achieving a bright smile, "if there is anywhere near here where we can get lunch. These children are starving!"

Mrs. Pummett looked at the two children, who gazed earnestly back at her; she looked at Mrs. Beewater's expensive, well-cut clothes, her stylish hat, up-to-date shoes and real leather hand-bag; finally she looked at her tear-stained face and her mind was made up.

"There isn't really anywhere here, except, I suppose, you could get bread and cheese at the pub——"

"Oh, yes," breathed Rose.

"... but if you would be content with what I've got in my house, I'd be very pleased—if you'd just come in—I mean, bacon and eggs and a pot of tea, and some bread and butter—would that do?"

The children's eyes flew to Mrs. Beewater's.

"That is very kind," she murmured graciously. "We shall be very pleased to accept your invitation. We all had an early start, and now, dear me, it is nearly half past two. Come along then, children, and then we must think about getting back."

As the procession walked across the grass to the cottage, Mrs. Pummett introduced herself and Mrs. Beewater introduced the children but did not mention her own name; indeed she did not have much time to do so as Mrs. Pummett was so busy explaining that her cottage was a very small one and everything in it was very simple, but clean she was sure, and they were very welcome to anything she'd got.

Richard and Rose were now chattering eagerly. Everything on that sunny afternoon had suddenly become delightful. They had seen but never before actually trodden on a real village green surrounded by old cottages and timbered houses with ivy-covered walls, with the church and rectory in one corner, the pond and its willow trees in the other. Even Mrs. Beewater felt her spirits rise, and she forgot, for a fleeting second, the failure of her mission and the hopelessness of the future.

Mrs. Pummett ushered them into the cottage and busily showed them up the steep little wooden staircase to a tiny bathroom, fetched clean towels and a new cake of soap, and told them to make themselves at home, while she flew to her frying-pan. In no time, while Ricky and

Rose were peeping into what presumably was Mrs. Pummett's bedroom, and Mrs. Beewater was thankfully sitting down in the crowded front room, a delicious smell of frying bacon began to fill the little house, and a cracking and a spluttering announced the addition of numerous eggs.

"I could eat an ox," sighed Rose.

"Me an elephant, hide and all," said Ricky, sniffing appreciatively.

"Come along now," cried Mrs. Pummett, in an incredibly short time. "You sit there, dear; and you here, and you, Mrs. Er, will this chair suit you?"

"Thank you," said Mrs. Beewater. She turned to Mrs. Pummett as she sat down. "I have never in all my life met such kindness. Such a meal at a moment's notice for three strangers!"

"Oh, well," said Mrs. Pummett, "I couldn't just leave you sitting there, you crying and all. Well, I said, there must be something wrong, I said to myself. How do you like your tea dear?"

It was not long before Mrs. Pummett and Mrs. Beewater were deep in conversation, while the children, having finished their bacon and eggs, were busily engaged in eating slice after slice of brown bread and honey.

Mrs. Beewater had naturally enquired after the Reverend Rupert Allendale.

"It was very sad," said Mrs. Pummett. "The poor old man! Everyone loved him, you know, but he should have retired years ago before he got quite so old——"

"How old was he?"

"Oh, all of 87, I should say. And though we all tried to look after things at the Rectory, they got into such a state. And the garden and all. Then he fell in the church once during morning service, and of course his duties in the parish got neglected too. Not his fault, poor old gentleman."

"Of course not," murmured Mrs. Beewater, her face

very sad.

"In the end Mrs. Winscombe wrote to his niece in America. Ever such a nice person. And she came over. She was very fond of him, and when she saw how things were, she got going and she and Mrs. Winscombe packed everything up, and she took him back with her."

"Did he mind, do you think?" asked Mrs. Beewater in a low voice. Her eyes had filled with tears. When you are old, she was thinking, it doesn't matter whether you mind or not.

"I think he was glad, because he must have known he couldn't cope. And he was very fond of this niece, you know. She was very kind——"

"Was she kind? Or just well meaning?"

Mrs. Pummett stared.

Mrs. Beewater tried to make herself clear. "I mean, was she kind to *him*? Or did she make him feel he was a nuisance who had got to be looked after?"

"I don't think it was like that at all," said Mrs. Pummett slowly. "As I say, she was very kind."

"Have you heard from him since?"

"He wrote once. A letter to everyone, you know, and it was read out in church."

"Did he seem happy?"

"Oh, yes. Very happy, I should say."

The conversation lapsed and Mrs. Pummett remembered her duties as hostess and offered more tea all round. The children were sitting quietly, leaning back contentedly, glutted with food. Mrs. Pummett excused herself and came back bearing a large home-made fruitcake which she cut into huge slices.

"No, no indeed, thank you!" said Mrs. Beewater, waving the plate away. "Richard, Rose, *ought* you to eat any more? Well, hurry up then! Goodness, it's a quarter to four!"

"It's the most super meal I've ever had," said Richard, stretching luxuriously.

"Me too," said Rose, still eating cake.

"I've loved having you," said Mrs. Pummett, beaming. "We don't see many strangers here at Little St. Paul's, and it's made a nice change. You must come again."

"Oh, yes, please," said Rose, chasing crumbs round her plate. She gave Mrs. Pummett one of her rare beautiful smiles.

Then as Mrs. Beewater began gathering up her handbag and gloves, Mrs. Pummett remembered there were several things she wanted to know. She turned to Mrs. Beewater. "You very badly wanted to see Mr. Allendale?"

"Yes. I wanted advice."

"Oh dear! Is there anyone else who would do? There is a vicar in the next parish."

"No, no!"

"There's Mrs. Winscombe. We all go to her when we're in difficulties."

"Who *is* Mrs. Winscombe?"

"She's a widow. Lived in Little St. Paul's all her life. Her husband was killed in an accident a month after they were married."

"Dear me. How sad. Well, no—I don't think Mrs. Winscombe could help me. You see..." Mrs. Beewater hesitated. One did not discuss one's private affairs with a complete stranger, but then this stranger had been exceptionally kind. "I too am a widow, and I haven't anywhere to live, and I thought if I could talk it over with Mr. Allendale..." Tears filled her eyes again.

Mrs. Pummett clucked sympathetically. "Oh dear! Well, Mrs. Winscombe——"

"*Not* Mrs. Winscombe, thank you," said Mrs. Beewater, firmly. "Come along, children. Thank you again so very much, Mrs. Pummett. May I reimburse you for this raid on your larder? No? But really, are you sure? How *very* kind you are!"

She was longing to be gone now, to be alone with her thoughts, the better to face up to the bitter fact that her scheme, on which she had placed the full weight of her hopes, had failed. Lucky Rupert Allendale, to have a niece who cared! Her eyes misted over as she looked through the little front door of the cottage, across the bright village green.

She stepped, as she thought, over the awkward, old-fashioned door-step, stumbled and fell, full length, in the porch.

The pain was terrible. For a moment she lost consciousness, and it seemed to her that she lay abandoned for ever with the dizzying pain swirling through every part of her. It was even worse when they tried to pull her to her feet, and she begged them to leave her alone. "I can't move," she moaned.

Mrs. Beewater was by no means a big person but, falling awkwardly as she did in the middle of the narrow doorway, it was no easy matter to know how to help her. Mrs. Pummett and the children raced out through the back door, round to the front of the cottage, and there they did their utmost to pull her to her feet. But poor Mrs. Beewater—her real leather handbag lying open on the path, its contents scattered, her hat lying upside down under a bush—cried out with pain. They could not move her.

Mrs. Pummett thought rapidly. She sent Rose to fetch cushions and a rug from the cottage, telling her exactly where to find them. Then she turned to Richard, pointing. "You see that white house there, standing out a bit? When you get to it you'll see it has a blue front door, and it's called Butts Cottage. Run as fast as you can and say, 'Mrs. Winscombe, please come at once to Mrs. Pummett. There's been an accident.' Hurry now!"

Richard and Rose immediately did as they were told. Rose was very soon back with the cushions and rug, and she and Mrs. Pummett made Mrs. Beewater as comfortable as possible in the circumstances. Mrs. Pummett did her utmost to remember what she had been taught about treating patients after an accident: Make them comfortable; keep them warm; treat for shock and collapse; and —of course—give them hot, sweet tea.

Richard meanwhile was tearing hotfoot round the village. He found Butts Cottage without any trouble, but Mrs. Winscombe wasn't at home. The front door was ajar and he pushed it open and shouted, "Mrs. Winscombe", but she didn't come. A neighbour popped her head over the wall and said, "She isn't there, dear."

"I know," said Richard. "Where is she?"

The woman looked curiously at Richard with his neat grey shorts and open-necked blue shirt. "Who wants her?"

"Mrs. Pummett. There's been an accident."

"Oh, my goodness! Mrs. Pummett's had an accident?"

Richard became imperious. He looked very like his mother. "Will you tell me, please, where Mrs. Winscombe is?"

The neighbour smiled. "Well, that I couldn't, dear. You know Mrs. Winscombe. No, you *don't* know Mrs. Winscombe." She paused to give Ricky an opportunity to say who he was and what he was doing in Little St. Paul's, and when he didn't oblige she went on, "She's always doing this or that."

"Where can I find her?" broke in Ricky desperately.

"She did go across the green some little while back. See that shop right over there? With the sign? Sells everything. She might be there."

Ricky was off like a flash, running hard across the green. Soon he realised that Mrs. Winscombe's neighbour was pounding after him. She was youngish and strapping and determined to be in at the death, as it were.

The bell of the all-purpose store pinged furiously as he shot in, gasping "Mrs. Winscombe?" The girl behind the counter stared. "Pardon?"

"There's been an accident at Mrs. Pummett's," explained the neighbour, taking over. "Where is Mrs. W.?"

"What sort of accident?" asked the girl, still staring.

"Never you mind," said the neighbour. "She come in here, dint she?"

"Not this afternoon, she dint."

Ricky turned towards the door, but the neighbour, who knew her village, said, "I know. Come with me." And she was off again, the bell still jangling violently, Ricky finding himself thankful for her lead. He was now extremely hot and breathless, and he wondered if this strange nightmare would ever end. Down a cinder track, down a little grassy lane, through some little flowery gardens... Somebody was coming out of a doorway, a woman plump and pleasant, with a fresh complexion and curly grey hair.

"Mrs. Winscombe," panted the neighbour. "Mrs. Pummett wants you. She's had an accident."

The first thing that struck one about Mrs. Winscombe was her serenity. She never flapped. After a steady look at Richard, she turned calm blue eyes on the neighbour, "What has happened?"

The neighbour looked at Richard, who returned her glance with one of dislike, although he knew very well he had some cause for being grateful to her. "Mrs. Pummett hasn't had an accident. It's an old lady," he said. "She's fallen and we can't get her up."

"What old lady?" demanded the neighbour.

"Never mind who it is," said Mrs. Winscombe, adding firmly (she knew her neighbour very well), "Thank you, Mrs. Jones. Now I'm sure you're busy and want to get back home, and the less fuss there is the better."

Dismissed, Mrs. Jones turned slowly away towards the shop as being the best place in which to gossip, while Mrs. Winscombe and Ricky walked quickly across the green to Mrs. Pummett's cottage. On the way, with very little prompting, he told her as much of the story as she needed to know.

CHAPTER 13

In the train going back to London, Richard and Rose found themselves sitting silent with a great deal to occupy their thoughts. Richard, looking at his watch, wanted to know what Rose was going to say to explain their late return. Rose shrugged her shoulders. "Mummy won't mind. I said in my note that we were going to spend the day with Helena."

"Another thing, Rose. Who is going to let the home know that Mrs. Beewater is in hospital. She won't be able to."

"Oh! I hadn't thought of that!" said Rose, sitting up and taking notice. "We don't know the number. D'you suppose she'll ask Mrs. Winscombe to telephone from the hospital?"

Ricky shook his head. "She won't think about things like that at present. Perhaps later she may."

Once more they fell silent, seeing over again Mrs. Beewater's fall, her lying helpless in the doorway, crying with pain until the doctor came (sent for by Mrs. Winscombe) and gave her an injection. After which the ambulance had arrived and two men had lifted her on to a stretcher and had driven her away to hospital, accompanied by Mrs. Winscombe. Rose thought tearfully of that. She had so wanted to go too so that Mrs. Beewater would not be entirely alone among strangers, but Ricky wouldn't allow it, insisting that they must get home. He had complete confidence in Mrs. Winscombe.

It seemed almost impossible to believe that the events of the past few hours had been crowded into the space of one day, or that until that day they had never set eyes on the dear little village of Little St. Paul's, and had never even met Mrs. Pummett. Rose, in particular, felt she had known Mrs. Pummett all her life and was intimate with her friendly cottage with all its ups and downs and ins and outs. She longed passionately to go there again.

She leaned across to Ricky on the opposite seat.

"You don't think she'll die, do you?"

"Not die, no. Have her leg off perhaps. Mrs. Winscombe said she thought she had broken it."

"Oh, Ricky, no!" Mrs. Beewater with only one leg! It was not to be thought of.

They were running into London when they spoke again. Richard said, a teasing smile on his face, "I say, Rose, your prayers didn't do much good, did they!"

Rose thought. She replied seriously, "Well, I don't know. I think they did. What about Mrs. Pummett and that gorgeous lunch? Honestly, Ricky, I'd have *died* if I hadn't had something soon. I've never been so hungry in all my life!"

"Nor me. All the same..." He paused, thinking things out. "It was odd, wasn't it, Mrs. Beewater falling down. I don't know anything about God, of course. You say you do. Well, either He didn't care or—perhaps He let her fall down because you, and me too, of course," he added handsomely, "shouldn't have been there at all. I mean, we shouldn't have been, should we? I said all along Mummy would never have let us go because she said you weren't ever to see Mrs. Beewater again, didn't she?"

Rose looked at him, her eyes wide, her mouth open. She had no answer to that. For the first time the realisation of what she had done swept over her and she thought she would drown in her wrong-doing. Naturally, she had known perfectly well that she was disobeying her mother, but she had not let herself stop to think; she had not faced up to her actions, because she had wanted to go with Helena. And had God let Helena fall because of

Rose's disobedience?

"We'll have to tell Mummy now," Ricky went on, "after what's happened. We can't just keep quiet about it, because for one thing she will have to phone Haven Hill."

"Couldn't we phone from the station?" faltered Rose.

"No, we couldn't," said Ricky flatly. He was tired of being the man of the family; he wanted to hand the responsibility over to older and wiser people, whatever the consequences. The day seemed to have gone on for ever.

Though Rose had been severely jolted by what Richard had said in the train, she was entirely unprepared for the storm that had been brewing at home. Their mother met them in the hall, a massive figure of wrath: she looked seven feet high. "Where have you been?"

Rose fumbled and looked at Richard, but he wasn't helping her. "We—I left a note. We've been with Helena."

"Mrs. Beewater, you mean?"

"Y-yes."

"Where?"

"In S-Sussex."

"Richard, go up to your room. At once. Rose, come with me. You've asked for it, my girl, *and you're going to get it*. Didn't I tell you that you were not to have anything to do with the Steele family, not even with the old grandma?"

Ricky had stopped half way up the stairs. He said loudly, "Mrs. Beewater has had a very bad fall and probably broken her leg. That's why we are so late. We wouldn't have been otherwise."

"It's just too bad Mrs. Beewater has broken her leg, but being late isn't really what matters. It's your defying me, Rose. Your deliberate disobedience. I'm easy with you, I know (*go to bed, Richard*) and you think I don't care, but this is too much!"

Seizing Rose by the arm she propelled her first to the little room beside the front door where she did her accounts, and, having extracted a cane from the drawer, dragged her up the stairs to Rose's bedroom. And there, with Rose face down across the bed, she used the swishy cane with great effect.

"Don't   you—ever—try—those   tricks—on—me—again!" said Hilda Runnall, driving home the lesson with vigour.

Rose's screams filled the house.

When it was all over Rose lay in bed, her face pressed into the pillow, unable to stop crying. It wasn't only her mother's terrible wrath or the horrible cane, though both were good cause for tears; it was the worry over Mrs. Beewater as well, the fear of what would happen to her and whether they would ever meet again, the hopelessness and helplessness of youth with its lack of experience. She was still only nine though Richard had now turned twelve, and it seemed to her then that she had sunk into such a deep pit that she would never see daylight again.

And why hadn't Ricky been beaten? Dimly she realised that mothers are usually tenderer with their sons than with their daughters, but she was honest enough to admit that it was she who had been disobedient, not Ricky, and that it was she who had engineered the plot and carried it through. All the same her mother didn't know that and hadn't even given herself time to find out the facts. Resentment surged through her.

Ricky meanwhile had thought very much along the same lines and sat shivering on his bed wondering whether his mother and the cane would visit him also. When he heard her going downstairs he relaxed with a sigh, undressed and put on his pyjamas and dressing-gown. Then with considerable courage he went downstairs to face his mother.

Jack had turned down the television but the picture

was still showing, and every now and then, while Hilda was talking to him, he stole a look at it. The family drama had occurred, awkwardly enough, during one of his favourite programmes. It was at once clear to Ricky that his mother's wrath had nearly subsided. Only once or twice before could he remember her in a rage and she had soon got over it. She stopped in the middle of a sentence as he gently turned the handle of the door and came towards her.

"You," she said. "And what do you want?"

"About Mrs. Beewater—no, listen, Mummy! This is important. She's in hospital and the home they put her into don't know. Will you phone them? Mummy, don't argue! Somebody's got to tell them."

Hilda Runnall looked at her son, and her gaze softened.

"What *are* you talking about, Ricky?"

Patiently, Ricky told her as much of the story as he thought necessary, making it very clear that Rose and he had accompanied Mrs. Beewater to Sussex not, indeed, for fun but because Mrs. Beewater would otherwise have been alone and very unhappy.

"You may telephone if you wish," said Hilda Runnall at length.

Ricky fetched the directory and hunted through the H's and, as he had feared, the number wasn't listed under Haven Hill. He looked hopefully at Jack.

"I don't know Madame's name, so what do I do?"

Jack took the telephone book and looked again under Haven Hill, Havenhill, and Homes. It wasn't there.

"Much as I hate suggesting it, you could phone Mrs. Steele," said Hilda. "I did try earlier but she was out."

"They're all in Scotland."

"Really, Ricky! Why ever did you have to get involved? All this fuss. Anyway, I can't make head or tail of the story. And why don't the home know about her? And," she finished, with a return of her wrath, "why should *you* care?"

"Hilda!" exclaimed Jack, reproachfully, adding unexpectedly, "The boy is right. He can't just leave it. Obviously the home don't know because Mrs. Beewater has had an accident and is not in a fit state to tell them. But listen, Ricky, why don't you try phoning this Mrs. What's-It at—what's the name of the village? Look, get Directory Enquiries and have a paper and pencil handy. She may have got the address of the home from Mrs. Beebrook."

"Beewater," corrected Ricky, laughing with relief.

"Ridiculous name for any woman to have!" muttered Hilda.

The upshot of it all was that Hilda Runnall had her first conversation with Mrs. Winscombe and was very much impressed. Yes, Mr. Beewater had asked Mrs. Winscombe to get in touch with Haven Hill and she had found the telephone number in her handbag. Yes, it was now definite that Mrs. Beewater had fractured her thigh, and it looked as if she would be in hospital for some little time. She was in less pain now though and as well as could be expected, and why didn't Mrs. Runnall bring those two darling children down to see her a little later on when she was feeling better? "Well, why not?" said Hilda, and took down the address of the hospital. She became quite her old self, full of good humour and camaraderie.

"But tell me," said Hilda, "what about the daughter, Mrs. Steele? Will she be coming down from Scotland?"

"I don't know," said Mrs. Winscombe. "The matron of the home was in rather a flap—well, naturally—and had let Mrs. Steele know her mother was missing, and I think she was going to get the first plane back to England. But did you ever? When the cat's away ...! Quite an enterprising old lady, don't you think?" The two women laughed happily down the telephone wires, and Ricky could scarcely believe his ears.

When his mother had replaced the receiver he said

simply, "Now I'll go and tell Rose and get her some supper."

And so the storm, terrible while it lasted, blew over,
but two conversations, upstairs and down, went on well
into the night. While Ricky fed Rose and himself with
cold chicken and ham, and bread and butter, and apple
tart, and cheese, and pop, and chocolate biscuits, he told
her of their mother's astonishing conversation with Mrs.
Winscombe.

"*Really* do you think Mummy will take us down to see
Helena?" pleaded Rose, her tear-swollen eyes beginning
to shine.

"Well, Mummy seemed to be getting on like a bomb
with Mrs. Winscombe, and if we play it cool perhaps they
would take us to Little St. Paul's and the hospital on
Saturday. You never know."

"Oh, goody," sighed Rose, putting down her knife and
fork to hug herself.

Downstairs Hilda and Jack Runnall were having a
most unusual conversation—unusual for them, that is.
Jack was saying what he thought, and in four years of
married life Hilda had never once heard him express a
firm opinion on any matter of importance. Hilda didn't
even know he could think, yet here he was saying, "You
know, Hilda, it's all very well ... those children are absolutely marvellous. The way they don't get themselves
into trouble, I mean. Because, after all, what bringing up
do they get?"

"What?" said Hilda, startled.

"They're alone all day. When they're not at school, I
mean. They're left entirely to their own devices."

"Jack! That's not fair! Evenings and weekends—we
give them lovely weekends. They have everything they
want. Money and everything."

"Too much! But they haven't any grown-ups to take
an interest in them. I know Mum is always here during
the day, but I don't suppose the children take any notice

of her. And I'll tell you something she said to me once: 'Them kids need looking after. I'm paid to run the house and I can't do everything, and what they get up to I *don't* know.' "

"She did, did she!" exclaimed Hilda indignantly. "Impudence!" She was thinking that that was almost what Margaret Steele had said, and also her first husband, Richard Anders. The children had been the cause of many rows between them. He had said that, while Ricky and Rose were small at least, Hilda must stay at home and look after them, but Hilda had argued that while she liked having children she had no intention of turning nursemaid. Business was her natural element and was as necessary to her as the air she breathed. Richard Anders had bitterly resented this and at last they had quarrelled irrevocably; he had gone from her for ever and now had another wife and family. The trouble was, she thought, they all wanted to force her into a mould that was too small for her. She would not have thought of not being married, she would not have liked to go childless, but the life of a housewife, with (in her opinion) its dreary routine of cooking and shopping, housework and the endless wants of children, would have driven her dotty.

While Hilda was thinking these things Jack was also thinking—or perhaps remembering is a more accurate way to describe the process, Jack not being much given to thought. His own old mother had always been *there*. She was not, he supposed, a very clever woman. She had never been taught anything about the correct way to bring up children, she just knew how to do it; and when you had a problem it was dear old Mum you went to. She made the home. Jack could smell again the warm smell of cooking, and when you came home from school or work there was Mum ready and waiting, all neat and fresh and welcoming.

But these poor kids! Really Hilda was awful! She hadn't any idea of what children needed. Got everything they wanted indeed—they hadn't anything! Not that Jack was complaining for himself. The easy way, the comfortable life was what he had always looked for and Hilda suited him very well. She was vastly capable, not demanding, a good companion, and his life was run for him with no effort on his part. But the children, poor little things, were another matter.

Hilda felt his eyes upon her and there was a look in them she had not seen before. Criticism, even resentment.

"I've never had children of my own," Jack said, "but I'm fond of your kids, Hilda, and I'd hate to see them go wrong. And they will, you know. When they are a little older there'll be plenty of people, the wrong ones, who will take an interest in them if you don't."

Hilda made no reply. But later, much later, when Jack had finally turned off the television, and they had had their late night drink, she said abruptly, "I have made up my mind. They must go to boarding-school."

CHAPTER 14

In the long, painful weeks that followed her accident, Mrs. Beewater had little to do but think, and her thoughts were seldom congenial. She felt disinclined to read or talk or listen to the radio, and certainly not to the other patients' chatter. She felt old and tired and ready for death—not that she wanted to die; the love of life was still strong in her, even at eighty years of age, but what sort of life could she look forward to? She searched every nook and cranny of her mind, trying to find a solution to the problem. And when she was tired of looking forward she inevitably looked back, and her memories made her sad, partly because the good times, she thought, had gone for ever, also because she had been brought by a series of unhappy jolts to look at these good times with a critical eye and to see herself in a very harsh light. Sometimes she cried a little, silently, the tears rolling slowly down her cheeks.

One day Mrs. Winscombe came in (as she often did) unnoticed, before Helena could rub the tears away. She sat down beside her while Helena fumbled for her hand-kerchief.

"Tell me," she said quietly, her kind, calm eyes showing sympathy.

Helena shook her head. "There's too much to tell."

"Is your leg hurting?"

"That is the least of my pains. I could put up with that!" She had found her handkerchief and had put her face to rights with a series of dabs. And now she smiled. "It's good of you to come. Tell me some more about the village."

They chatted for a few minutes. Then Helena said, "It's strange. I came several times with my husband to Little St. Paul's but I never met anyone except the Rector."

"I am surprised I didn't see you in church. In a small village like ours you can't miss visitors."

"We didn't go to church," returned Mrs. Beewater shortly. She remembered her husband's good-natured chaff at the beliefs held by his boyhood friend, the gentle Rupert Allendale. Mr. Beewater had had no use for religion.

"Has Mrs. Pummett been again?" asked Mrs. Winscombe at length.

"She was in yesterday, and I told you Mrs. Jones came."

Mrs. Winscombe nodded and smiled. Though the hospital was six miles away from the village, Mrs. Jones would certainly not have missed visiting its latest celebrity. And in her loud, funny way she was kind. "She brought me some flowers. Those over there. You know, it really is incredible."

"What is?"

"The kindness of everyone. When we visited Mr. Allendale we never bothered about the village or anyone in it, and yet when I'm in trouble the whole of Little St. Paul's take an interest in me and tries to help ... and Mrs. Pummett even before the accident——"

"She's one of the kindest people on earth," commented Mrs. Winscombe.

"She must be! You never saw anything like the meal she rustled up at a moment's notice for me and the two children, and she wouldn't take a penny for it."

Mrs. Winscombe laughed. "I think it gave her great pleasure to be able to entertain you. She thought Richard and Rose were wonderful—you too, Mrs. Beewater."

"Me? Impossible! Why, the first time she set eyes on me I was in tears!"

"I know," said Mrs. Winscombe gently. "She thought you were so brave."

"I certainly wasn't," said Mrs. Beewater, shaking her head, remembering over again the utter despair of that sunny afternoon on the green when she knew that her last hope had gone. "Isn't life strange? Little St. Paul's for me used to be a peaceful, quiet place where only peaceful things happened, and now—an unpleasant shock and a still more unpleasant accident ... Shall I ever walk again? Mrs. Pummett said you used to be a nurse, so you should know."

"I don't see why you shouldn't. With a stick probably, at first. It will depend to a great extent on your determination and perseverance. Have you many stairs at home?"

"I haven't got a home," said Mrs. Beewater, turning away her head. "For the last few months I have been living with my daughter. I used to have a flat in Kensington."

"I see," said Mrs. Winscombe. So that was the trouble. "Mrs. Steele is your daughter, isn't she? Is she the only one?"

"I have a son."

There was another silence. Mrs. Winscombe then said, "Is your daughter coming down from Scotland to visit you?"

"Not until they have finished their holiday. I told Matron to insist that it wasn't necessary, but I believe she has telephoned Matron every night!"

"I suggested to Mrs. Runnall that she should bring the children to visit you while you are in hospital."

"Oh! What did she say?"

"She seemed quite agreeable, as far as I could judge. I don't know her, of course."

"I don't either. I have barely set eyes on her. She is the managing director of a series of shops, you see, and is hardly ever at home."

"The poor children! What do they do?"

"You may well ask. It worries me. They are left so much to their own devices, and that is how they came to be with me at Little St. Paul's when I had my accident. They shouldn't have been, you know, and I do hope there was no trouble."

"There didn't appear to have been," said Mrs. Winscombe comfortably. "The mother seemed quite happy when she rang. She sounded friendly."

"I don't think she's quite that," said Helena drily. She went on, "You see, Rose and Richard too were so anxious about my coming here all on my own, and they—Rose, that is—insisted on looking after me. Rose, for some reason which I can't quite explain, has taken me under her wing. I think it's because she is lonely."

And because you are lonely too, thought Mrs. Winscombe. You both feel unwanted. She nodded encouragingly and Mrs. Beewater went on talking about Rose; and then she went further and began to talk about herself. Mrs. Winscombe listened intently while she described, with horror, homes for old people, The Homestead and Haven Hill, and frowned as she realised the fear of the future which possessed the old lady.

"I can see it's a terrible problem for you." Mrs. Winscombe, her chin in her hand, studied Mrs. Beewater's strained and anxious face. "I suppose your daughter hasn't really room for you," she ventured.

Mrs. Beewater stared at the pale green wall opposite without seeing it and after a long silence said, "No."

"It seems to me that it wasn't by chance you came here," Mrs. Winscombe observed.

"What do you mean?"

"Things don't happen by chance."

"I should never have come. Even young Richard advised against it!"

"But you did come. And you'll be here quite a long time, as things have turned out."

"And so?" queried Mrs. Beewater doubtfully.

"And so for the moment we needn't worry. We must just leave it and take a day at a time."

"How kind of you to say 'we'. I feel better already, knowing that you are in this with me!"

"Of course I'm in it with you!" said Mrs. Winscombe warmly. "But more than that: I'm going to pray about it, and do you know what that will mean?—that God is in it too! Tell me, Mrs. Beewater, do you believe in prayer?"

"Well..." said Mrs. Beewater. She thought earnestly before continuing, "I never have prayed until recently. It's never been necessary, you see. I've had everything I wanted or needed until my husband died."

"But have you prayed recently?"

"Yes."

"And what happened?"

"It worked," answered Helena, with a little laugh.

"I believe very much in prayer," said Mrs. Winscombe matter-of-factly. "I don't think I could live without it— that is, not without God to pray to. Now look, we'll make a pact: we'll both pray—you here, me at home—about your future. God still works miracles, you know, and this won't be beyond Him."

"What shall I pray?"

"You must discover that for yourself," said Mrs. Winscombe, and she took her leave, promising to come again the following afternoon.

It was not until the little hospital was settling down for the night that Helena began thinking seriously of what Mrs. Winscombe had said. *It wasn't by chance you came here.... We needn't worry.... Do you believe in prayer? I do.* 'What shall I pray?' *You must discover that for yourself.* But how could you discover it? She could not find the words or the heart to pray as she lay sleepless in the semi-darkness of the ward. Then the words of the twenty-third Psalm slowly took possession of her thoughts:

'The Lord is my shepherd; I shall not want. He maketh

me to lie down in green pastures: he leadeth me beside the still waters. He restoreth my soul: he leadeth me in the paths of righteousness for his name's sake.... I will fear no evil: for thou art with me ... Surely goodness and mercy shall follow me all the days of my life: and I will dwell in the house of the Lord for ever.'

How she came to know the words of the Psalm by heart she could not imagine. If Minnie Barnes had taught them to her she did not remember her doing so, but there they were leaping to life after years of neglect, and she found them comforting. What were the paths of righteousness? Where were they? 'I shall not want.' Why shan't I? Presumably because *He* is my shepherd. But is He? If so, I have been a very troublesome sheep! Never once, all my life long, have I ever followed Him or asked Him to lead me.

And so, with these thoughts running through her mind, she drifted into a peaceful sleep and awoke in the morning happy, the words still running through her head: 'I shall not want.... He leadeth me in the paths of righteousness.'

CHAPTER 15

Dear Mrs. Beewater, my dear Helena,

How are you getting on? Are you still in bed, I do miss you, I do *wish* I could see you. Probly next term weer going away to school, Ricky and I. Mummy told us. Rickys rather fed up but I think I'm pleased.

Do you have many visitors, I wish I could come.

Love,
Rose.

Rose had thought quite a lot before she had written to Mrs. Beewater. She was not sure whether she ought to write, not only because she did not want further trouble with her mother, but because she saw very clearly that unless she had permission it would be a further act of disobedience to have anything to do with the Steele family. She took her problem to Ricky, who thought the matter over carefully before saying, "You can't just not have anything to do with Mrs. Beewater. It would be most frightfully hurting to her, because she can't possibly know that Mummy has said you're not to. And you can't just abandon someone who's in hospital with a broken hip."

"Certainly not!" agreed Rose fervently.

"Well, I think all you can do is ask Mummy if she minds you writing."

"Ooh, Ricky—I can't!"

"Come off it, stupid! She's not angry now, is she?"

"N-n-o."

"Well, then."

"But supposing she says no?"

Ricky had to admit that that would produce a very tricky situation. He himself was sincerely fond of Mrs. Beewater and, although he did not miss her as Rose did, he still could not bear the idea of just leaving her to her fate after all that had gone before. He said, "Look, we'll both go to Mummy about it, but you'll ask her if you can write because you're the one who was warned off her. If she agrees, O.K., I won't say anything. If she refuses I'll remind her of her telephone conversation with Mrs. Winscombe when she practically said we could go and visit her."

"Oh, yes, Ricky, do! Oh, Ricky, I do love you. But will you ask her anyway if we can go and see her?"

"If you have any sense you'll go one step at a time," said Ricky, turning away.

A favourable opportunity came that evening. Supper was over, Jack was contentedly watching television, Hilda was sitting back comfortably, enjoying a cigarette and the evening papers.

Rose went and stood in front of her mother, giving Richard a kick as she passed his chair.

"Mummy."

"M-m?" said Hilda, not raising her eyes from the paper.

"Mummy, listen!"

Hilda put down the paper, frowning a little, and saw her daughter's rather white face, solemn and anxious, a mute appeal in her large eyes, and she smiled slightly. "What's worrying you, darling?"

The unusual term of affection brought a slight colour to Rose's cheeks and she also smiled. "Mummy, I wanted to ask you if—if—may I please write to Mrs. Beewater? Please let me, Mummy. She's in hospital and may be there for a long time." Rose twisted her hands together as Hilda stared at her.

"What an extraordinary child you are, Rose! Whatever sort of a hold has this old woman got over you?"

"She hasn't got any sort of a hold over me," retorted Rose, nearly in tears. "I—she—I just love her, that's all."

Richard was watching warily from his chair, and even Jack had for a few seconds removed his eyes from his television. Hilda was aware of this and possibly it made a difference.

"At least you've asked," she conceded grudgingly, "which is quite something. All right, Rose. You can write to her if you want to, but mind, I'll have no truck with the Steeles, or with those two kids of theirs. Understand?"

"Oh, yes," agreed Rose promptly, adding meekly, "I won't have anything to do with the Steeles." It was easy enough to promise that!

"You handled that pretty well," Richard told her as they were going to bed.

"I did, didn't I?" said Rose, glowing.

So the letter was written and posted and Rose could only wait for the answer in a fever of impatience. When it came she read it over and over again: once alone, locked in the bathroom; once to Ricky; once rather falteringly to her mother, hoping she would seize on the suggestion of a visit (which she did not), and thereafter whenever she thought of it.

The Steeles by this time were home from their holiday in Scotland, and Margaret had paid one flying visit to her mother. She reported favourably to her husband on her return.

"Really, Robert, if she hadn't fractured her thigh you could very well say she had fallen on her feet! She is in a very nice little ward and seems happy, and for some *unaccountable* reason she has a *host* of friends. They visit her and bring her flowers and do bits of shopping for her, and quite seem to have taken her to their hearts."

"So now you can relax," said Robert, "which is a relief, let me tell you!"

"I don't see how I could have been expected not to

worry," complained Margaret. "So far away and unable to do anything——"

"Except run up enormous telephone bills!"

"Don't be so *niggardly*, dear. Telephoning every night was cheaper than a return air-fare from Scotland. She is my *mother* after all!"

And anyone would think you were fond of her, thought Robert. He said, "Did she explain how she came to be in Little St. Paul's?"

"She said, but very vaguely mind you, that she had gone to visit the Rector there—Mr. Allendale. You wouldn't know him, but he was a friend of Father's. I couldn't really make head or tail of the story."

"Mentally confused, perhaps?"

"Oh dear, no! Not *Mother*. She simply had no intention of explaining. You know her. She just likes to go her own way, and this time it has landed her in trouble."

"From your point of view she seems to have made a very wise move."

"Robert!" protested Margaret, unreasonably, having said almost the same thing herself. "At the moment, of course, I *am* relieved of worry, but what will happen when they want to discharge her from hospital?"

"I can't possibly look so far ahead. It will depend to a great extent, I should have thought, on whether she will be able to walk. But let's not think about it now."

Half-way to the kitchen Margaret paused and returned to the lounge. Her husband sighed and rustled his newspaper irritably. "What, Margaret?"

"Don't you think we ought to go down and see Mother on Saturday? All of us, I mean. I think Jennifer and Marilyn *ought* to see her."

"You take them then. I've got to—er——"

"No, Robert, *you* ought to see her too. We'll have an early lunch . . . I'll phone the Matron." And having settled things to her own satisfaction Margaret went off contentedly to do her cooking.

Saturday was bright and cheerful, an ideal day for a drive. Margaret, happy and at peace because she was doing the right thing, and everything was working out just as she had planned, sat in front of the car with her husband. who, having no rooted objection to visiting his mother-in-law, was quite enjoying taking his wife and daughters out for the afternoon. Jennifer and Marilyn sat at the back, well-dressed and well-behaved, two little young ladies on a grown-up outing.

As they drove through the hospital gates, Margaret said, "Now, Jennifer and Marilyn, Granny won't be able to see too many visitors all at once, so I want you to stay quietly in the car for a few minutes while Daddy and I go in; then if she is well enough you can just run in and say how d'you do."

Jennifer and Marilyn placidly agreed.

Margaret made her rather majestic way to the little side ward, Robert following meekly in her wake. At the door she paused uncertainly, hearing voices and laughter in which she recognised her mother's. "She seems to have visitors already." Stiffening, her head erect, she marched in, and the voices and the laughter ceased abruptly as she confronted the group round Mrs. Beewater's bed: Hilda Runnall, a man whom Margaret rightly assumed to be Mr. Runnall, and a woman with grey curly hair and blue eyes.

Mrs. Beewater immediately took command of the situation, saying graciously, "Margaret, dear, how nice. And Robert too. I don't believe any of you have met——" And with several waves of her hand she introduced them all.

Margaret Steele and Hilda Runnall acknowledged each other distantly. "And, Margaret," went on Mrs. Beewater, "I particularly want you to meet Mrs. Winscombe. She has been so very kind."

At this juncture Richard and Rose joined the party, somewhat breathless, having run at top speed all round the hospital ground.

"Hullo!" said Rose, pulling up her socks, her eyes growing wide at the sight of her mother and Mrs. Steele together at Mrs. Beewater's bedside. "I thought you must be here," she said, addressing Mrs. Steele. "We've just seen Jennifer and Marilyn outside in the car."

"Yes, I told them to stay there quietly," said Margaret repressively.

Then the ward sister swept in, her eyes blazing. "What is the meaning of this! One, two, three, four ... seven people round a patient's bed! This I cannot allow."

"It was quite unintentional," said Mrs. Winscombe placatingly. "The last four have only just arrived—Richard. Rose, come with me," and with an arm round each child's shoulder she hurried them from the room. Outside in the corridor she began to laugh. "Poor old Sister Turner! That will be enough to keep her awake all night. Now listen to me, children. I suggest you all come over to Little St. Paul's and have tea with me—no, I'll tell you what: you two can have tea with Mrs. Pummett. She'd love to see you again."

"But the Steele girls are here too. Jennifer and Marilyn. Outside in the car," explained Rose.

"Well, we can phone Mrs. Pummett, then she won't be taken too much by surprise. The grown-ups can come to my house. I badly want to meet them."

Rose looked imploringly at Richard who so far had said nothing.

"You see," said Richard, "it's a bit awkward. Mummy and Mrs. Steele don't much like each other."

"Aha," said Mrs. Winscombe gravely. She had been very much aware of the sudden drop in temperature at the Steeles' arrival, and had not been able to account for it.

"And we can't take Jennifer and Marilyn to tea with Mrs. Pummett because Mummy won't let me have anything to do with them," rushed in Rose.

"Oh dear," said Mrs. Winscombe. She thought the matter over for two seconds, then nodded her head. "Leave this to me. You two go outside—we really mustn't upset Sister Turner any more—and then we'll go and phone Mrs. Pummett, and you can come back in the car with me and help to get tea ready."

"But—but I want to see Mrs. Beewater," said Rose, her face clouding over.

"Don't fret, Rose, this is just a beginning," said Mrs. Winscombe. "It's just too wonderful they have all met here. Now things will be better, especially after they have all had tea together, and you'll be able to come down again—for a weekend perhaps."

"Do you think so?" queried Rose doubtfully.

"Sure of it. And if you went in now, Rose, with all those grown-ups there, you wouldn't get a word in edgeways!"

That was true enough! But Rose felt rebellious and resentful. The whole visit to Mrs. Beewater had been planned chiefly for her benefit and here she was being hustled outside like the two kittens in the nursery-rhyme. But one had a sort of feeling about Mrs. Winscombe: if she said Leave it to me, you did leave it to her, knowing she wouldn't make a hash of whatever it was. She turned and followed Richard down the smooth corridor to the front door.

Mrs. Winscombe joined the little crowd beside the bed. Margaret Steele and Hilda Runnall were sitting on the two available chairs, the men were standing with their arms folded, and Mrs. Beewater was giving them a lively and amusing account of her sufferings. Mrs. Winscombe stood quietly by until she saw her opportunity.

"It's just after three o'clock," she said, seizing a lull in the conversation, "and I have a suggestion to make. Little St. Paul's where I live is about six miles from here, not more, and I would like you all to come and have a cup of tea at my house."

The women were quick to protest: "So kind, but really no..."

"The children, you see, can have tea with Mrs. Pummett,' continued Mrs. Winscombe, unperturbed. "Richard and Rose, and your two little granddaughters, Mrs. Beewater, while you all come to me." She smiled at the two couples in turn.

Margaret gave in gracefully. "Well, thank you; a cup of tea would be very welcome, wouldn't it, Robert?"

But Hilda was not so easy to persuade. She loved organising but hated being organised. "It's very kind of you, Mrs.—Er——," she said firmly, "but really not. We have other arrangements."

"I do rather want to see you," said Mrs. Winscombe in a low voice, her blue eyes fixed on Hilda's, and with a blink Hilda capitulated. After all, Margaret Steele would never know of the embargo she had laid upon Rose, so she wouldn't lose face. "Very well," she said.

Mrs. Winscombe ran off to telephone Mrs. Pummett; the Steeles and the Runnalls presently withdrew; and, under the nose of the longsuffering Sister Turner, the four children came and stood round Mrs. Beewater's bed for a minute or two. Jennifer and Marilyn dutifully kissed her forehead, Richard said politely, "I hope you're feeling better, Mrs. Beewater", while Rose said precisely nothing. She simply stood, her arms hanging limply at her side, and stared at her beloved Helena. When it was time to go she turned and left without a backward look.

CHAPTER 16

The tea-parties proceeded merrily. After receiving Mrs. Winscombe's telephone call Mrs. Pummett had dashed across the green to the village shop, where she purchased two of McVitie's iced cakes (four children? That should be enough with the scones I made this this morning), and scurried happily round her kitchen thinking loving thoughts about all dear children and what a pleasure it was to feed them.

Mrs. Winscombe, having given careful directions as to how to get to Little St. Paul's, went on ahead in her car, Richard and Rose with her, hoping her guests would follow in due course. She had made more sure of this by saying privately to Margaret, "I would so much like to talk to you about Mrs. Beewater", and to Hilda, also privately, "If there's a moment I would like a word with you about Rose and Mrs. Beewater."

The guests did follow her, and, in her long, charming room with wide windows at both ends of it, sat chatting amiably about this and that while Mrs. Winscombe dispensed tea. When she went to the kitchen to replenish the tea-pot Hilda slipped out after her, pushing to the kitchen door with her foot.

"What about Rose?"

Mrs. Winscombe carefully put down the tea-pot and faced the hard, handsome businesswoman, with her impeccable clothes and perfect hair-do. She smiled.

"Perhaps I am interfering. It's just that I have become extremely interested in Mrs. Beewater and Rose. And they are so devoted to each other."

"I know. I'm not sure that it's healthy."

Mrs. Winscombe raised her eyebrows. "Oh?"

"Well, their ages, for one thing. Nine and eighty-five."

"Eighty."

Hilda shrugged.

"I don't think age comes into it," said Mrs. Winscombe. "It's a matter of minds. They fit. But the thing is, they pine for each other, and I think it will do Rose harm to be deprived."

"You seem to have learnt a lot in a very short time," said Hilda sharply.

"Yes," returned Mrs. Winscombe simply.

"So what do you suggest?"

"Let her come and stay here every now and then while Mrs. Beewater is in hospital. Richard too, if you like. Either with me or Mrs. Pummett. We'd love to have them."

"They are going to boarding school."

"So I gathered. But not yet, I believe."

A burst of laughter from the three in the other room brought a scowl to Hilda's face. She turned on her heel and left the room, saying briefly, "I'll think about it."

Later, when the tea was over, Margaret helped Mrs. Winscombe to carry the things out to the kitchen. "You have been so kind to my mother."

"I have become very fond of her."

"I am afraid she is a bit demanding."

"No. She is wonderfully patient and takes everything as it comes. But let me come straight to the point, Mrs. Steele. She is worrying about her future. It's a terrible anxiety to her. Do you know that?"

"Yes," said Margaret, unhappily, gazing at her feet. "But what can I do? It isn't a good idea her living with us, and I can't find a suitable home for her. Even the very expensive ones aren't what she wants."

"She dreads the idea of a home."

"I know."

The two women gazed at each other. "Will you think I am interfering if I try to help her?" asked Mrs. Winscombe.

"I'd be only too thankful if you would," Margaret responded. "But—how can you? I mean..."

"I don't know," said Mrs. Winscombe slowly, busying herself at the sink. "But one thing I am sure of: Mrs. Beewater may be old in years but she is not senile—not childish—so we mustn't treat her as if she is. *She* must make the decision about what she will do."

"Ye-es ... but——" began Margaret, uncertainly.

"We must help her to make the right decision."

"Oh, if only you would!" cried Margaret. "I'm absolutely *desperate*." Tears filled her eyes. "But what *is* the right decision?"

"I've said I don't know—yet. It's a big problem. First of all, I think we ought to have a word with the hospital social worker and ask her to find out about how long she will be immobile, etc. Now you live a long way off; would you like me to make preliminary enquiries?—on your behalf, of course, and I would keep in close touch with you."

Here Robert Steele appeared at the door. Not finding the Runnalls very much to his taste he had come in search of his wife. He was surprised to find her beaming with joy. Without another word being said on the subject, the care of Mrs. Beewater had passed from her daughter to her friend.

While the five grown-ups were drinking tea and having earnest discussions at Mrs. Winscombe's house, the children were having a hilarious time in Mrs. Pummett's cottage. Rose, having quite recovered from her disappointment, was in the highest spirits at being in her favourite village once more, with Mrs. Pummett's lovingkindness enveloping her like a warm, fragrant blanket.

"Oh, Mrs. Pummett, I do love you," she cried, hugging her round her dumpy little waist.

"Yes, dear, but just let me make the tea, there's a love. Look, you take these scones in and put them on the table and then come back and I'll have the honey ready for you. Have your two little friends washed their hands?"

"You bet!" said Rose, laughing contemptuously. They had, and were standing neatly by the window of the front room gazing across the green. Soon, however, they and Richard found Rose's exuberant spirits infectious, and, as they drank their tea and demolished the two cakes and all but one of the scones, the four children joked and laughed and told stories and nearly rolled under the table with mirth. In fact, the two little Steeles, rarely being allowed out on their own apart from going to school, were enjoying themselves hugely, and to Rose's astonishment she even caught them laughing with their mouths full.

Then all too soon their father's green Rover drew up outside the window, they hastily swallowed their last bits of cake, and, smiling politely, thanked Mrs. Pummett very much for having them, stood by dutifully while their mother thanked her effusively, and sat quietly in the back of the car while their father drove rapidly towards the London road.

"Did you have a nice time, chickabiddies?"

"Yes, thank you," they chorused.

And then the incredible happened—and without too much trouble!

When the Steeles had left, Hilda and Jack Runnall visibly relaxed. Hilda sat down again and lit a cigarette. Jack produced his pipe.

"You've got a nice place here," Jack said, nodding at the view across the green. "You like the country?"

"I love it," said Mrs. Winscombe. "You could say the village is my life."

"You should have heard my children," said Hilda, now comfortably sprawling in the big chair. "Rose especially couldn't say enough about Little St. Paul's."

Though not to you, my girl, thought Jack. She never dared mention Little St. Paul's to you! It was to Mum she talked endlessly about the glories of country life.

Mrs. Winscombe smiled appreciatively. "They will have had a lovely time with Mrs. Pummett. She has a gift with children and..."

But Hilda wasn't interested in Mrs. Pummett. She switched the conversation back to herself and Richard and Rose, much to Mrs. Winscombe's secret satisfaction.

"You see, I'm in a difficulty with those two kids. I have to work—well who doesn't these days—so they have to more or less look after themselves, don't they, Jack? And they're pretty good, I must say. Level-headed—you know —but I've decided it's time they go away to school, then there would only be the holidays to worry about."

"When will they go?" murmured Mrs. Winscombe.

"When I can get them in and no sooner. Not this coming term, of course. Sometime next year, I should think."

"And how do they feel about it?"

Hilda shrugged. "It's just one of those things. Oddly enough, I think Rose quite likes the idea."

"Not Ricky, though," said Jack.

"I wonder why he doesn't," said Hilda, a little irritably. "Anyway, he'll have to go, like it or not. I can't have him alone at home, and the sooner Rose is integrated in a female community the better." She saw Jack looking at his watch. "Yes, we must be going."

"You will remember about Rose coming to see Mrs. Beewater?" suggested Mrs. Winscombe gently. "Let them both come and stay before they go back to school."

Still sprawling, Hilda looked fixedly at Mrs. Winscombe for a few seconds. "They can stay now, if you like," she said carelessly.

"Hilda!" exclaimed Jack.

"Why not?" said Hilda, stubbing out her cigarette. "If Mrs. Winscombe thinks the village can contain them!" She smiled engagingly. "My husband thinks I'm being rude and I probably am! But I mean, no time like the present. They are here now and there's nothing special for them to do at home until they go back to school. So why not?"

"A splendid idea," said Mrs. Winscombe briskly. "As you say, no time like the present. But what about clothes and so on?"

"Neither of them cares particularly what they wear in the day-time, but they should have pyjamas, I suppose. And a toothbrush. There's a shop over there on the green, isn't there? Do they sell that sort of thing?"

"They sell everything."

"There you are then." Hilda removed several pound-notes from her purse. "They can go and get the things they want. O.K. by you, Mrs. Winscombe?"

"Absolutely," said Mrs. Winscombe.

At the end of the day when Little St. Paul's lay quietly with the lights of the houses clustered round the green glowing warmly through the summer darkness, Mrs. Winscombe walked across the sweet-smelling grass to Mrs. Pummett's cottage. There she found Rose dressed in her new pyjamas being plied with cocoa and biscuits in the front room.

"I somehow thought I'd find you in bed," Mrs. Winscombe said, looking kindly at Rose.

Mrs. Pummett was inclined to be apologetic. "She did go to bed once but she couldn't sleep——"

"Too excited," said Rose between loud gulps of cocoa.

"The cocoa'll settle you down," said Mrs. Pummett comfortably. 'Drink it up, lovey, and then we really must say goodnight. We've got all tomorrow, remember."

"Lovely," sighed Rose, shutting her eyes and pretending she would wake up and find her incredible turn of

fortune had been a mere dream. "Isn't Richard *silly*?"
she demanded. "But I think I'm pleased. I'd rather be
here on my own actually."

Richard, in fact, had refused to stay, and nothing his
mother could say could make him. "I will not be pushed
around," he repeated quietly but stubbornly, and had
got into the car and sat there until at last Hilda, flushed
and angry, had given up the struggle and Jack had
driven them away. At first Rose had been upset, and
then, afraid that she would not be allowed to stay without him, had run into Mrs. Pummett's little back garden
and hidden behind a bush.

When Rose had finally gone to bed and Mrs. Pummett
had climbed the steep, narrow stairs to 'settle' her in the
little, awkwardly-shaped room with its sloping roof and
old-fashioned wash-stand, the friends sat down for a cosy
cup of tea, as they frequently did at the end of the day.

"Why do you suppose Richard refused to stay?" asked
Mrs. Winscombe.

"If you ask me," returned Mrs. Pummett, "she handled
it wrong! I really couldn't blame him. That woman!"
she muttered wrathfully.

"I know!" said Mrs. Winscombe.

The next morning Rose woke to find the oddly-shaped
little bedroom flooded with sunshine, and she immediately jumped out of bed to pull the curtains and see her
dream village for the first time in the morning light. It
seemed to her that the sun always shone in Little St.
Paul's. Just then the church bells began to ring and she
realised it was Sunday, and after breakfast she and Mrs.
Pummett went to the morning service. Most of it was
double-Dutch to her, but she liked it. She liked the peace
of the little old church and the gentle light filtering
through the stained glass windows; she liked the organ
and the singing of hymns, and, kneeling between Mrs.
Pummett and Mrs. Winscombe, she watched them as they
followed the prayers and made the responses, marvelling

at their quiet, reverent attitude. As yet she did not know the meaning of the word 'reverent'. This was something quite outside her experience, and she felt she had entered into another world, a peaceful place where the struggles of life could not enter in. As she sat on the hard wooden pew the sermon seemed long and she scarcely understood one word the visiting preacher said, but even so she would not have cut it short by a single minute.

And then in the afternoon—oh, joy and delight!— Mrs. Winscombe drove her to the hospital to see Mrs. Beewater, and left her alone with her for half an hour while she went to visit another patient in another ward.

At first Rose was tongue-tied. She had so much to say that words would not come. Then Mrs. Beewater said, "Life is strange, isn't it, Rose? Who would have thought that you and I would be together here—me in hospital and you at Little St. Paul's?"

"You didn't think this was going to happen when you used to come and see Mr. Allendale with your husband, did you?"

"I certainly never did! Mrs. Winscombe thinks that nothing ever happens by chance and perhaps she is right. I have a feeling that I have come to a turning point and nothing will ever be the same again."

"Do you think things will be better? Or worse? I mean, what do you think will happen now, when you're better?"

"I am just not worrying about it, Rose. That is the first thing that is different. Do you know the twenty-third Psalm?"

"That's the one about the Good Shepherd, isn't it? Yes, we learnt it at school."

"That's it. Well, it says, do you remember, 'He leadeth me beside the still waters.' I feel I'm just there now, content to stay by the still waters until God moves me on; and do you know what else it says? 'He leadeth me in the paths of righteousness for his name's sake.' "

"What does that mean?"

"I am not sure. I suppose it means He leads me in the right way. The Shepherd is looking after the sheep and so the sheep doesn't have to worry about which way to go."

"You know," said Rose, "I think God must be most awfully kind."

"I am beginning to think so too," said Mrs. Beewater.

Rose stayed the whole of that week in Little St. Paul's and she had never in her life been so happy. The village took her to its heart. Everyone knew her story and what they didn't know they made up, and she became one of themselves. The children played with her and showed her their treasures and listened to her stories about London. She helped Mrs. Pummett with her housework and visited with Mrs. Winscombe and came to know quite a bit about the needy people in the village; she took Mrs. Jones's dog for walks and even was even allowed to sell things in the village shop. She visited Mrs. Beewater three times.

The sun did not always shine in Little St. Paul's. One day it was very wet and on that day Mrs. Pummett taught her how to make scones and let her bake some apples in the oven, and in the afternoon, after she and Mrs. Pummett had polished the furniture together, they settled down to do a jigsaw puzzle.

"I don't ever want to go home," sighed Rose.

"Oh, I think you do, dear," said Mrs. Pummett reprovingly. "There's no place like home, you know."

Rose considered this. "No place like my home certainly, but that doesn't mean it's a nice place."

"Rose, dear, that's not very kind. What would Mummy do if you weren't there?"

"Just go on working," said Rose promptly. No need to think about that one! But then she added, "I do want to see Ricky, of course."

"Of course you do," agreed Mrs. Pummett. "He's your

brother and a dear lad too. I expect he's missed you."

"You never know," said Rose, and Mrs. Pummett decided to change the subject. She felt very sad.

"But don't think I shan't miss you, Rose, because I certainly shall," she said at length.

Rose looked up at her, a long searching glance. "Will you? Will you *really* miss me, Mrs. Pummett. So can I come back?"

On the Saturday morning when Mrs. Pummett and Rose were tidying up her room in readiness for her to be collected by her mother and Jack that afternoon, Mrs. Pummett suddenly said, "Look, Rose, I'll pop these sheets in my neighbour's washing-machine, like I always do, and when they are dry, look, I'll put them in this drawer, see this bottom one, and I'll keep them specially for you."

"Oh, yes," said Rose, smiling with pleasure, her cheeks a little pink. "Yes, and you could put these in too." She held out her pyjamas. "And my talcum powder and sponge. Then they'll be ready for when I next come. I'll take the toothbrush though, because the one at home has all its bristles coming out."

CHAPTER 17

The weeks followed one after another very quickly. Richard and Rose went back to school, and then at half-term, when they had a week's holiday, they both went to stay at Little St. Paul's, with Mrs. Pummett. Rose loved having Ricky there; there was so much to show him and so many people to introduce him to. It was her village by that time and she was kindly letting him stay in it.

Mrs. Beewater was still in hospital but working hard at her physiotherapy ("Fizzy *what*?" said Rose the first time she heard the word) and beginning to walk quite long distances in the ward. The second time the children visited her they found their own way to the hospital by bus and brought two boxes of fried chicken and chips to eat in the little park near by, because, although it was nearly November, the weather was quite fine and warm.

"I am greasy!" said Rose, licking her fingers and rubbing them vigorously on the screwed-up ball which had once been a paper serviette included in the box of chicken.

"Rub your hands on the grass," suggested Ricky, and she did so, then stood on her hands, expertly waving her legs in the air until she fell flat on her back, where she lay for quite a minute gazing up at the blue chasms of sky between the clouds, thinking how happy she was.

She sat up suddenly. "Ricky!"

Ricky, lying stretched out on the wooden seat, said "What?"

"You do see now, don't you, that, when we prayed on the green at Little St. Paul's, God did hear and do something. Well, He did, didn't He? I mean, just look at everything which has happened since, Mrs. Beewater so happy, and Mrs. Winscombe looking after her, and us staying with Mrs. Pummett, who we'd never have met unless Helena had cried on the seat under the tree——"

"Oh, Rose, don't run on so! Yes, well, I agree things took a turn for the better that first day in Little St. Paul's, and if you want to give God the credit for it I don't mind one way or the other. Only don't keep harping on it."

"Helena thinks as I do," pursued Rose, hugging her knees and rocking backwards and forwards. She wanted passionately to make Richard understand, not only to prove her point that God had indeed heard and answered her prayer, but to make him know what she now knew about God, and about His Son, the Lord Jesus Christ, the Good Shepherd who gave His life for the sheep.

"You think you know all about God, don't you?" said Ricky. "You talk as if He were an intimate friend of yours!"

"He is, He is!" cried Rose. "I'm not a very good Christian—"

"Ha, ha, ha," said Richard, but he wasn't laughing.

"—yet," finished Rose. "But I will be one day. You know Miss Sooling at school. She teaches Scripture and she's ever so interesting. I used not to like Scripture. I used to think it was boring; most people in my form think that. But it's not, not when you know what it's all about, and when you know that Jesus came back to life again and is *still* alive, I mean *really* alive and wanting to help you. Miss Sooling says that Jesus came down to earth to be a man so that we would understand what God is like, because we'd never have understood otherwise. Miss Sooling says that the Bible tells you all about it, and that if you read it you can see for yourself. Helena doesn't know much, you see, because she has never read it, but after all she did give me that big Bible with the pictures in it, and I love that!"

"When you grow up you'll have to join the Salvation Army or the Jesus People," said Richard.

"I might too," said Rose seriously.

There was a great deal more she would have liked to discuss with Ricky, but in the first place she could not have put into words the vast thoughts which were filling her mind, and secondly Ricky didn't want to know. She could sometimes talk to Miss Sooling at school but there wasn't often much time and anyway Rose often felt quite dumb. But dumb or not she had the mighty facts of the Christian faith firmly fixed in her mind and heart. She *knew* that Jesus Christ had died on that terrible cross because she had done wrong (her disobedience over Mrs. Beewater, for instance; her bad temper; the many times she had not told the truth—'sins' in fact) and that because He had died God could forgive her. She *knew* without any doubt that He had forgiven those sins, and many others beside, because she had asked him to forgive and she could feel in her heart that He had. Rose, at ten years of age, was no theologian, and she could not have explained how these things could be: she simply believed and in due course the Holy Spirit in her heart would help her to understand.

The children wandered off towards the hospital.

Mrs. Beewater was sitting in the armchair beside the bed, her transistor beside her. She looked very well and seemed happy though she did admit that she was getting a *little* tired of hospital life.

"But, do you know," she said, "I can walk quite a bit now and Mrs. Winscombe has invited me to go and see her at home! I don't think I could get in her car yet but the hospital have a sort of ambulance with a platform that goes up and down so that it can take people in wheelchairs. And Sister Turner thinks they could take me while they are picking people up in Little St. Paul's and call for me when they return them after treatment. It's all got to be arranged, of course. But tell me, what is Butts Cottage like? Is it a house or a cottage?"

"A house," said Richard. "Not a very large one, I mean not *very* large, but it's not all that small either."

"Is it an old house?"

The children were doubtful. "M-m, well. It's not as old as some of them in Little St. Paul's but it isn't modern."

"It isn't like anything you'd see in London," volunteered Rose, whose knowledge of London was not extensive. She meant that it was not a typical 'London house'. "It has a garden, back and front, and crazy-paving paths, and at the back there's a place where you can sit in the sun without feeling the wind—not a verandah; like a sort of built-in terrace. Mrs. Winscombe has lots of her meals there. Sometimes even in the winter!"

"Who looks after the garden?"

"She does mostly, the plants and things, but an old man from the village comes in to cut the grass and sweep up the leaves."

"We had a super bonfire there," said Richard, "down at the bottom of the garden in a sort of little hedged-in place. I love bonfires."

"Me too," said Rose. "We put *everything* we could find on it and it burnt and burnt, and then when it was dark it was all red and glowing and when Ricky poked it a lot of sparks flew out!"

"Does Mrs. Winscombe like gardening?"

"Oh, yes, she loves it. She says if she had her way she'd do nothing else. It's not work, she says—what's the word she uses, Ricky?"

"Relaxation," supplied Ricky.

"It's a pity you won't see it in the summer," said Rose.

Rose was desperately anxious to spend Christmas at Little St. Paul's but it could not be arranged, in spite of all her pleading.

"No. Once and for all, no, Rose," her mother told her.

"And don't let me hear any more about it. I don't understand your always wanting to rush off to that mouldy little village. Christmas is a time when families ought to be together. What about Jack and me?"

"What about Jack and you?" demanded Rose rebelliously and rather rudely.

"Doesn't it occur to you that we may want you and Ricky to keep us company and come out with us? Jack has taken a lot of trouble to arrange things, and I do think, Rose," Hilda complained, "that you might be a little appreciative!"

Rose sulked for a few seconds then conceded grudgingly that it all sounded lovely, and suddenly, with something of a shock, Hilda realised for the first time that Richard and Rose were growing up—Ricky twelve now, Rose ten—and soon they would be making their own lives and she would be left alone with Jack. She herself was not far off forty and she gazed with a certain amount of foreboding into a bleak future. She hadn't had time for the children when they were young; they wouldn't have time for her when they were older. Already they were showing signs of going their own way...

From then on Hilda tried to be nicer to Rose, more friendly, more interested in her affairs.

So Christmas came and was soon over, and Hilda and Jack carried out their programme of entertaining the children and having a good time themselves.

At Little St. Paul's life was also merry and very busy. Mrs. Pummett was far from well, having had flu, and Mrs. Winscombe found time to run in and out of the cottage, and on Boxing Day she called for both Mrs. Beewater and Mrs. Pummett and brought them home for lunch and tea.

"Have you got any further?" Mrs. Pummett had opportunity to whisper to Mrs. Winscombe.

Mrs. Winscombe shook her head. "I haven't heard yet.

Maybe the letter has been delayed in the post. She promised she would let me know before Christmas, and I do wish she would get on with it."

"So what does the hospital say?"

"Naturally they keep on pressing for Mrs. Beewater's discharge but Mrs. Steele emphatically refuses to have her home, even temporarily. Well, there are all those stairs, of course, but she is walking quite comfortably now."

"I do think it's too bad. The poor old lady. She must be very hurt."

"I don't think so. She has no wish to return to her daughter. I must say she seems perfectly serene."

"Will they send her to a Council home?"

"I believe the social worker did try to put her name on a waiting-list but you have to wait ages for a vacancy, and anyway she refused to go. And the Steeles' pride would prevent it if nothing else did."

"She must have been in hospital nearly four months."

"Yes, and it has been good for her, I think. Everyone has made such a fuss of her, even the doctors, and she spends a lot of time in the big ward now, talking to other patients and doing odd jobs for them. Mrs. Steele simply can't believe it!"

Mrs. Beewater also was waiting for a letter, and a week after Christmas it arrived. It was from Mr. Allendale's niece in America. She wrote:

I am afraid you will be sad to hear that my uncle died just over a month ago here at my house. But please try not to be sad. He was happy to go. You probably know that he had an unshakeable belief in an after-life, and in his last few minutes—he was conscious almost to the end—he said gently and peacefully. 'In my Father's house ... I shall soon be there. He is keeping a place for me and He will be coming to fetch me.' It makes such a difference, doesn't it, when you know that someone you love has not gone out into darkness or nothingness and that you will meet again.

Mrs. Beewater was indeed very sad at first. She put the letter away in her handbag among her other precious possessions, and only brought it out to show Mrs. Winscombe.

"I wish he had known I was at Little St. Paul's," she mourned, "and that I came to see him and to ask his advice. If only I had written sooner!"

"Perhaps he does know," ventured Mrs. Winscombe. "We can't tell, but I don't think you must let yourself grieve about it, Mrs. Beewater. It was through him you came to Little St. Paul's and you must thank God for that—or at least, *I* thank God for it!"

"Me too, as Rose would say," sighed Mrs. Beewater. "Everything happened very strangely, didn't it. On the face of it, I should never have come here, or let the children come. I was pig-headed, I know, and you might say my accident was a punishment, though I can't regret it. But now, Mrs. Winscombe, if you have got a few minutes I absolutely must talk to you about my future. The social worker was here again yesterday and she keeps on saying that I can't stay here. The doctors are agitating for my bed."

"I came specially to talk about your future," said Mrs. Winscombe.

It happened that Hilda Runnall had been hoping for a letter too, though not actually expecting it. Ellernmeade School could now offer Rose Anders a place in the following term. The authorities were sorry to give such short notice owing to unforeseen events, but it would be appreciated if Mrs. Runnall would inform them at once if she wished to accept the vacancy for Rose. Mrs. Runnall wrote immediately accepting it. She then told Rose.

"In a fortnight's time?" said Rose.

"In a fortnight's time," agreed Hilda, matter-of-factly. "You wanted to go, didn't you, Rose?"

"Yes," said Rose slowly, in a small voice. "Yes," she said more firmly, "I do want to go. I'm rather glad it's all settled. Well, now, Mummy, I must go and say goodbye to Mrs. Beewater."

Hilda was at first irritated by this, until she remembered her new resolve 'to be nice to Rose'.

"There's not much time. We shall have to get you some clothes and all the whatnots the school requires—but I suppose it could be fitted in. It's a good job Richard isn't going next term as well."

"Richard says he isn't going—ever."

"Oh, *does* he! Well, he is."

Rose returned to the all-important subject of Mrs. Beewater, partly because she was afraid she had given Ricky away; also because she thought privately that, if it came to a conflict of wills between her mother and her brother, Ricky would win. He was more stubborn than the proverbial mule once he had made up his mind, and was quite capable of taking advantage of his mother's weak points. At all events, Rose did not feel able to fight his battles, she had enough of her own.

"Will you ring Mrs. Winscombe, Mummy? This evening? Promise?"

Hilda promised.

CHAPTER 18

A few days later Mrs. Winscombe met Rose at the junction with the car. Richard had firmly refused to accompany her to Little St. Paul's but he had volunteered to escort her to Victoria Station and put her on the train, and to meet her the same evening after her visit. Hilda had had one or two qualms about her travelling alone and Jack had certainly not approved though, as usual, no one had taken any particular notice of what he had said.

"What on earth can happen to her in just over one hour?" demanded Ricky. "She won't play with the doors and fall out. Will you, Rose?"

"No," said Rose.

"And you won't speak to strangers," said Hilda with a little frown and an odd little smile.

"Or accept sweets from them," mocked Ricky.

"No, *no*, NO," shouted Rose. "I'll sit like a statue all the way. After all, there's got to be a first time for everything, and I'm ten now."

All the same, she was glad Richard had put her on the train and would meet her on the return journey. Because sometimes things are a little frightening—even when one is ten years old.

Mrs. Winscombe's reassuring face was at the junction barrier to greet her and Rose felt a deep content sitting beside her in the car along the winding Sussex roads. She talked happily about her new school and Mrs. Winscombe listened attentively. That was one of the best things about her: she always listened and found what you said important. Presently at a road sign Rose broke off to say, "This isn't the way to the hospital."

"No," said Mrs. Winscombe, "I thought we would have lunch at my house."

"But——" began Rose. "It's very kind of you, Mrs. Winscombe, and don't think I'm being rude or anything——"

"But you came to see Mrs. Beewater and there isn't much time. I know, dear; but everything is well under control, and there's no need to worry." Mrs. Winscombe was smiling, almost laughing—what at, Rose had no idea.

As the car drew up at Butts Cottage she gave two little toots on the horn and before they had reached the front door it had opened, almost, it seemed, of its own accord.

"Helena!" cried Rose.

There she was, leaning on her walking-stick, her left hand held out in welcome, an old lady certainly (older perhaps since her accident and all those weeks in hospital) but looking very well and attractive, and smartly dressed in a new, red two-piece. Rose hugged her gently as something very fragile and precious.

"Come in!" said Mrs. Beewater, as if she owned the house, and she led the way, hobbling a little but walking quite steadily with the aid of her stick, to a room leading out of the long sitting-room with the windows at each end.

"Take your coat off, love. Oh, Rose, I *am* pleased to see you! I've been longing for this moment."

Rose looked about her. The room as quite large and had french windows opening out on to the terrace, with a lovely view of the garden and the country beyond. It was comfortably furnished. There was a divan bed in one corner with a handsome cover and several brightly coloured cushions; there was a table with a bowl of fruit on it and two or three chairs grouped round in a hospitable sort of way, and two armchairs by a modern gas fire, and a dressing-table with—Rose stared at it—Mrs. Beewater's silver-backed brushes and mirror and the photograph of her husband in its silver frame...

"Helena, are you staying here, or do you *live* here?"

Mrs. Beewater took Rose's coat and laid it gently on the bed, and with her free hand stroked Rose's cheek. "I live here, Rose. I came three days ago."

"You never *told* me," said Rose reproachfully.

"Don't be cross with me! I was longing to tell you, but—you see, everything happened at once. The hospital wanted my bed and there was nowhere for me to go, and although Mrs. Winscombe and I had talked about this quite a lot we couldn't fix anything because she was waiting to hear from someone—another old lady—to whom she had offered this room, but she just didn't write, and then at last she did write saying she had made other arrangements. Oh, the relief! But then it all had to be discussed with my daughter and I didn't dare tell anyone before it was all settled. Then when your mother telephoned about your coming to visit me, Mrs. Winscombe and I thought it would be fun to surprise you."

"You've certainly done that!" said Rose. "It's all too good to be true."

Mrs. Winscombe popped her head in at the door. "Lunch is ready. We are having it in the dining-room today, Rose. In fact I think we shall usually have lunch together, and Mrs. Beewater will be able to manage the rest of her meals on her own."

After lunch (a very good one, Rose thought) Mrs. Beewater took Rose back to her room and they sat by her gasfire and talked. It was a cold day and the room was friendly and warm. There was so much to say and time was short.

"Tell me about your school," said Mrs. Beewater. "You did go for an interview, didn't you?"

"Yes, Mummy and I spent practically a day there. It's in Hampshire, in the country, miles from everywhere, in a sort of large park with a wall all round it and iron gates at the entrance to the drive. Rather nice really. They have riding lessons and keep rabbits and things."

"What is the headmistress like?"

"All right, I suppose. But I don't expect I shall see much of her. There were one or two of the other mistresses around and they seemed quite nice. It won't be too bad. Anyway, I'll know more about it when I've been there, and of course I'll write to you. Let's talk about you now. Helena, will you like being here?"

"I can't tell you, Rose, just how much I like it. After all that unrest and misery and uncertainty, it seems—well, you remember what our Psalm says: 'He leadeth me beside the still waters.' I had a kind of conviction He would, you know. That just describes it: Still waters."

"It's a long way from Harrods and Kensington!"

"A very long way, but that doesn't worry me now, and I don't think I would go back if I could. This is my village now. I am getting to know everybody gradually and the more you know them the more interesting they are. It's fascinating. And they all seem to know me, already some of them call me Mrs. Bee—B–E–E. Rather homely, don't you think? Let's hope I don't develop a sting! I must be careful not to. I'm so happy it would be a pity to spoil it."

"What will you do all day?"

"Mrs. Winscombe and I have talked it all over very carefully, and we agreed that we wouldn't actually live together. We'd see a lot of each other and be good neighbours but lead our own lives. Look, Rose, you see my electric kettle, and my electric ring, and the little cupboard there with all my own china in it? I shall get my own breakfast when I'm ready for it and the odd cups of coffee, etc. and have my own visitors, and Mrs. Winscombe will cook for us both every day, so in the evening I shall only need an egg or something. And I shall make my own bed and keep the room tidy, and Margaret is going to bring me a television set and my bookcase and bureau—remember? They will fit in nicely over there. And I'll read and I'll sew and write letters, and when the weather is better and my hip is stronger I'll be able to go out and talk to people and get things from the village shop. And—perhaps—I shall be able to do a few odd jobs for Mrs. Winscombe."

"Perfect," sighed Rose. "What does Mrs. Steele think about it?"

"She's delighted, of course. It solves her problem, doesn't it, and I think, Rose, that we shall be very good friends apart. She will visit me every now and then— when she can get time off from her various committees— and she will go away again before we can get on each other's nerves. And I shall not feel I am being a nuisance to anyone, not even to Mrs. Winscombe, because, don't you see, it's a business arrangement. She has been wanting to let this room for a long time but couldn't get just the right person."

"You were the right person."

"I evidently was! Mrs. Winscombe told me that she had this room built on to the house some years ago for her husband's mother, and she looked after her here until she died, and most of the time since it has been more or less unused."

Rose smiled. "Waiting for you. Isn't it funny, Helena, when you think how you sat and cried on the green that day—you wouldn't have cried, would you, if you'd known it was all going to end like this."

Mrs. Beewater groped for her stick and got, rather laboriously, to her feet. On the wall beside her dressing-table was a little framed picture which she took down and brought over to Rose. It was hand-painted, a little watercolour of grass and trees and a lovely sunset, and across the blue and purple and pink of the sky were these few words: There is a God in heaven. Daniel 2.28.

Rose studied it in silence.

Mrs. Beewater said, "I saw it in Mrs. Winscombe's bedroom and I liked it so much that she gave it to me. Do you know about Daniel?"

"Daniel in the lions' den? Yes."

"Mrs. Winscombe explained to me that he was a member of Israel's royal family and he was taken captive to Babylon where he lived in the king's palace with three of his friends. And then one day the king had a dream which troubled him very much and he called his wise men and told them to explain it to him. But he either couldn't or wouldn't tell them what the dream was! So the king commanded that they were all to be put to death, Daniel and his friends among them. But Daniel managed to get the king to postpone the sentence for a time, and he and his friends prayed, and then God told Daniel in a vision what the dream meant and Daniel told the king, and explained to him that he hadn't done it of his own accord and that of course no man could, but, he said, There is a God in heaven who reveals secrets..."

"And Daniel's God is the same as ours."

"Exactly. So now, you see, I believe there is a God in heaven who heard me when I was in difficulties and made all these lovely arrangements for me."

She took the little picture from Rose and replaced it on the wall. "Rose dear, I am at the end of my life, or nearly, and until recently I have never even thought about God. He did not exist for me. I am sorry for that now. But you, Rose, you are just at the beginning of things. Don't make the mistake that I did: don't leave God out!"

The winter light began to fade. Mrs. Beewater turned on the shaded lamps in her room, and then switched on her electric kettle to make tea. They drank it almost in silence, beside the cheerful gas-fire, from Mrs. Beewater's own china, and then it was time to say goodbye.

On the way to the junction Mrs. Winscombe stopped at Mrs. Pummett's cottage and they ran in for a moment to see her. She looked very unwell, and, Rose thought, very old, but she was delighted by the visit and they parted with assurances that they would meet again during the

Easter holidays.

When the London train came in, Mrs. Winscombe
found a carriage in which there was a plump, kindly
looking woman with a teenage daughter. Rose sat by the
window on the far side and as the train gathered speed
she watched the lighted houses and the street lamps flying
by in the darkness. Presently there were no lights except
for an occasional twinkle through the trees or the head-
lights of a car, and Rose found that she was looking at
her own reflection in the dark window with the bright
carriage behind her.

With mounting excitement Rose, who as a rule took so
little interest in how she looked, continued to stare at
herself, thinking, this is me, Rose Anders, in a train all by
myself. I'm Rose travelling alone, I'm going to London,
and soon I'm going to boarding school, and then p'raps
I'll go to university, and then I'll marry and I'll have
children and a house of my own. And Helena will come
and stay with me and I'll look after her.

All the way to London she dreamed her dreams: Rose
Anders travelling through life. At Victoria station, feeling very tall, she walked along the platform to the barrier
where Richard was waiting for her, one small girl in the
hurrying crowd.